With her Beretta ████████████ **Gennie joined No**████████████ **SUV, where they hid in the shadows of tall pine trees and waited.**

There were no lights from the house behind the driveway and no other vehicles on the road. Raindrops splattered on the leaves and branches. The wind rustled.

If the vehicle that had been following them appeared, what should they do? An exchange of gunfire seemed like a really bad idea, especially since she and Noah didn't know who was in pursuit.

When she looked up at him, peering through the morning mist, his gaze locked with hers. "Thanks, Gennie, for putting up with me."

"I'm here for you."

He reached for her and pulled her into an embrace. Though layers of clothing and two Kevlar vests separated them, she felt his heart beating in time with hers. She wanted to tear off all these clothes, to race back to his cabin and snuggle up in a warm, cozy bed. But they had a job to do.

THE FINAL SECRET

USA TODAY Bestselling Author
CASSIE MILES

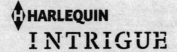

To Zinj, my latest feline grandson, and, as always, to Rick.

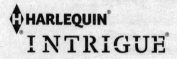

Recycling programs
for this product may
not exist in your area.

ISBN-13: 978-1-335-13632-9

The Final Secret

Harlequin Enterprises ULC
22 Adelaide St. West, 40th Floor
Toronto, Ontario M5H 4E3, Canada
www.Harlequin.com

Printed in U.S.A.

Cassie Miles, a *USA TODAY* bestselling author, lives in Colorado. After raising two daughters and cooking tons of macaroni and cheese for her family, Cassie is trying to be more adventurous in her culinary efforts. She's discovered that almost anything tastes better with wine. When she's not plotting Harlequin Intrigue books, Cassie likes to hang out at the Denver Botanic Gardens near her high-rise home.

Books by Cassie Miles

Harlequin Intrigue

Mountain Midwife
Sovereign Sheriff
Baby Battalion
Unforgettable
Midwife Cover
Mommy Midwife
Montana Midwife
Hostage Midwife
Mountain Heiress
Snowed In
Snow Blind
Mountain Retreat
Colorado Wildfire
Mountain Bodyguard
Mountain Shelter
Mountain Blizzard
Frozen Memories
The Girl Who Wouldn't Stay Dead
The Girl Who Couldn't Forget
The Final Secret

Visit the Author Profile page at Harlequin.com.

CAST OF CHARACTERS

Genevieve (Gennie) Fox—Retired from the Army Corps of Engineers after an ambush in Afghanistan killed part of her team and left her partially disabled, she's a new hire at ARC Security and determined to prove herself as a bodyguard.

Noah Sheridan—Head of field operations for ARC, he admires Gennie's physical skills and qualifications. Her naturally blunt manner isn't well suited to detective work, but she's a fast learner. And he needs her help when accused of murder.

Tony Vega—Second in command at ARC.

Dean Slocum—The murdered blackmailer dies with many dangerous secrets untold.

Kenneth Warrick—An arms dealer from Afghanistan, he betrayed Gennie's affections and might have sabotaged her team. Discovering him in Colorado is definitely bad news.

Mitch Murano—The self-proclaimed guru from Boulder has made a fortune from meditation and enlightenment. As he aims toward a new career in politics, he has secrets that must remain buried.

Chapter One

Her mission was clear: rescue the hostage.

Gennie Fox wasn't exactly sure how she'd accomplish the task but needed to act fast. According to her information, her backup was due to arrive in less than fifteen minutes, but she shouldn't count on them. Her background info indicated that they couldn't be trusted. She needed to rescue the asset before anybody else showed up. And the clock was ticking down.

She made her approach, creeping through the forested hillside outside an isolated two-story mountain cabin with a cedar deck jutting from the south end. Late afternoon sunlight glistened on patches of spring snow that had mostly melted and left the ground muddy. With her back pressed against the rough trunk of a Ponderosa pine, she observed. Two armed guards patrolled the perimeter of the property. She suspected there were others inside.

If she'd had access to a heat-sensing scanner, she would have known whether the hostage was being held upstairs or on the lower level. The scanner wasn't her only lack. She had no binoculars, no auditory surveillance devices and her assault gear left much to be desired. The eight-inch double-edged blade in a sheath attached to her belt was good for silent combat, but the handgun she'd been given was clumsy and untrustworthy. Gennie preferred a fifteen-round Beretta similar to the weapon she'd carried on patrol in Afghanistan.

Her unpreparedness extended to her clothing. She'd expected to be meeting for brunch at a trendy spot in the Highlands area of Denver and had dressed in a black leather jacket, olive green silk blouse, black slacks and lace-up sandals with two-inch heels. For this one-woman assault, she should have been wearing head-to-toe camo and steel-toed Dr. Martens.

When one of the guards peered in her direction, her adrenaline spiked. She ducked behind the tree, hoping that her black outfit would blend into the shadows. Her blond hair was covered by a green patterned scarf, and she'd turned up her collar to hide her face. Only her blue eyes stood out. She squinted and watched as the guard turned his head and moved away.

For the moment, she was safe. But she couldn't just stand here, waiting to be caught. She'd signed on to play this game, and she intended to win.

Holding the gun in her left hand, she drew her knife with the right. Mentally, she mapped her route to the house. Guards had been coming and going on the deck, which meant the sliding glass doors probably weren't locked. But the approach to that entrance offered little cover, and she wanted to stay hidden as long as possible. Bent over, she dashed from the forested area toward a clump of trees nearer to the front door.

Halfway, her sandals skidded on the mud, and she sprawled. Her quick reflexes compensated for her clumsiness. She sprang into a crouch, froze like a statue and checked to make sure the guards hadn't seen her. Then she ran. Her left ankle stiffened. She was injured. No time to worry about it now.

At the house she peeked through a window beside the front door, didn't see a guard. The door was locked, which was what she'd expected. She had a lock pick attached to her key chain and knew how to use it. In mere seconds, the doorknob twisted easily in her hand.

Inside the entryway she scoped out the spacious room with a natural stone fireplace at one end, a hall leading in the direction of the deck on the other and a staircase directly across from the entry. A guard appeared in the doorway from the hall. He looked surprised to see her, and she took advantage. Before he could raise his weapon, she pounced and slashed her blade across his throat. He fell. *Take his rifle?* She decided against it. Her handgun was better for fighting in close quarters.

Killing the guard had been necessary. He'd been in the way, and she needed to succeed in this mission. *Upstairs or down?* Trusting her instincts, she rushed to the staircase and ascended to the second floor where she expected to find bedrooms. The upstairs would be easier to defend than what she assumed was a more open floorplan on the lower level.

Directly across from the landing, she confronted a closed door. Was the hostage being held in that room? The other doors on both sides of the long corridor stood open with the exception of the door at the very end.

At the closed door, she pressed her ear against the wood and listened. From inside, she heard a drawer being closed, then a shuffling noise and the thud of heavy boots walking across the floor. Coming closer to her? She jumped back as the door swung open. A guy in a guard uniform raised his arm at right angles to his body and fired at her. He missed. Her aim was more accurate. Two direct hits. The center of his chest turned bright red. He crumpled to the floor.

The gunshots had alerted the other guards. From downstairs, she heard their shouts. Her best guess for the location of the hostage was the closed door at the end of the hall. As she sprinted toward it, a red-haired maid in a pink smock stepped through one of the open doors, holding a stack of folded linens. She gave a shriek and threw up her hands. *No weapon. Not a threat.* Gennie pushed her back and told her to take cover.

At the closed door, she tried the handle. Locked! No time for finesse, she crashed through, using her shoulder as a battering ram. Tomorrow, she'd have a bruise, but the injury was worth it if she completed her mission. She pushed the door closed behind her. After slipping her knife into the sheath, she held her gun with both hands for stability as she scanned the large room—a well-equipped home gym with a wall of windows and a wide balcony.

A tall lean man wearing knee-length shorts and a sleeveless T-shirt jogged on a treadmill, moving in time to music that must have been playing on his wireless headphones. His back was toward her. When he turned his head, she recognized his profile.

Without lowering her handgun, she approached. "Noah Sheridan."

With a glance in her direction, he stepped off the

treadmill, removed his headphones and rubbed his hand across his close-cropped dark brown hair. "Good timing, Captain Genevieve Fox. The van carrying your backup is pulling into the driveway."

She braced herself, expecting a twist at the last minute. "Are you the hostage?"

"Who else would I be?"

He came toward her with his hand extended as though to offer congratulations. But he hadn't followed the script. The information she'd been given stated that the hostage would introduce him or herself by saying, *Take my hand and set me free.*

Waiting for him to say those code words, she hesitated. *Big mistake!* He made the first move. A chop on her wrist, and she dropped her handgun. Before she could pull her knife from the sheath, he spun her around and swept her legs out from under her.

He could have ended her mission then and there. Her gun was within his grasp. His dark eyes blazed with excitement. She could tell that he wanted a fight, wanted to show her who was the boss. *Not going to happen.* Sure, he had the physical advantage. But she had the intense determination of ten combat-ready soldiers.

The door whipped open. The other guards arrived.

"Back off," Noah shouted to them. "I've got this."

Bite me! She scrambled to her feet, never taking her focus off Noah. If she subdued him, she had the advantage. Noah was the boss. The guards had to obey his orders.

When he grabbed her, she rolled backward, using his momentum to throw him off-balance. Regaining her feet, she thrust out her injured left leg as an obstacle. He tripped and fell to the ground. Avoiding his grasp, she went down on her knees behind him where she got him in a chokehold, pulled her knife and held it in front of his dark eyes.

He flicked the tip of the rubber blade. "I've got one thing to say."

"What's that?"

"You're hired."

The bodyguards, including those she had supposedly killed, swarmed into the home gym, applauding and hooting their approval. She counted five men and one woman—the non-threatening redhead who had been carrying a stack of folded sheets.

Noah pushed her rubber knife out of the way and stood. "How did you like our Rocky Mountain version of Hogan's Alley?"

Though she'd trained at Quantico, Gennie had never gone through the original Hogan's Alley—a famed FBI simulator exercise where actors and other agents took on the roles of villains and innocent bystanders. But she'd played the video game where thugs popped out from behind bushes and a nanny with a baby carriage was in the mix.

"To tell the truth," she said, "I wasn't expecting this kind of workout at my first job interview for ARC Security."

"That's the point. If you decide to join us, you need to be ready for action at any time and in any circumstance."

He took her hand and helped her to her feet in a gesture that might have been designed to make her think he was a gentleman. Most definitely, he was not. The fire in his eyes told her that Noah had enjoyed their hand-to-hand combat. He was competitive, and she had no doubt that if he'd thwarted her assault, he would have relished the victory.

She straightened her shoulders, pulled the scarf off her neck and ran her fingers through her chin-length blond hair in a futile attempt at grooming. Technically, he'd said that she was hired but she wouldn't feel comfortable until she signed a contract. Her confidence had taken a hit when she'd belly flopped into the dirt outside the house and ruined her silk blouse. Her injured ankle was another problem.

The fake guards surrounded her, offering congratulations and words of welcome. The lone woman among them had taken off her pink housemaid's smock. Her sleeveless top showed tanned well-toned arms. With that level of fitness, she was probably a field agent, and Gennie was glad. For much of her life, she'd been in situations where women weren't an equal part of the equation. From military engineering courses at Texas A&M to boot camp to two and a half tours of duty, she seemed to be always proving herself against a male standard.

The ARC crew seemed friendly, especially the guards she'd "killed" with her rubber knife and paintball gun. A handsome guy with a killer smile introduced himself as Tony Vega. "I'm the thug you knifed in the entryway. How'd you get inside so fast?"

"Picked the lock."

"Nice move." When he bobbed his head, he reminded Gennie of her younger brother. "You got skills."

"But I failed the mission," she said. "I didn't rescue the hostage."

"Because there was no hostage," Tony said.

Noah explained, "This scenario was an ambush, designed to capture you. The information we gave you hinted that you couldn't trust your own people. When I attacked, your instincts kicked in. You overwhelmed me but didn't kill me. Smart move. You could use me as a bargaining chip when my men came into the room."

"Is this the usual exercise?" she asked.

"We change it every time," the woman said. "Otherwise, we'd get bored."

"And we're all grateful," Tony added, "that you went upstairs instead of charging into the kitchen and messing up the barbecue we've got planned. Hungry?"

Noah interrupted. "The rest of you go downstairs. I've got some paperwork for Gennie."

Smiling, she watched them leave. Their friendly camaraderie reminded her of her platoon in Afghanistan, which was what she'd expected when she applied at ARC Security, also known as Noah's ARC. They mostly hired ex-military personnel and had a stellar reputation as bodyguards, crime solvers and bounty hunters, as well as the original ARC Security Division that dealt with computers and cyber-crime.

"Come with me," Noah said.

She followed him down the hall, walking carefully on her injured ankle. He held open the door to the first room on the landing where she had encountered a guard. The space was furnished with bookshelves, cabinets, a desk and several computer screens.

"An office," she said.

"This is actually my house," he explained. "The location is convenient, less than an hour out of Denver. When I'm in town, I have a condo."

"You don't mind messing up this house playing war games with paintball splatter?"

"Bachelor," he said as if that explained everything. He gestured to a long sofa at the base of the bookcases. "I have a few questions for you."

Gingerly, she lowered herself onto the clean-line sofa. "I'm still hired, right?"

"I want you working for us. As soon as I saw your résumé, I knew you had the right stuff. You worked security in Kabul in Afghanistan, is that right?"

"Only occasionally," she said. There were times when they'd wanted a woman as a bodyguard, and she'd been available. "Between my tours of duty, I trained at Quantico."

"You have contacts in the FBI and the army," he said. "That's a plus. Several of our contracts are with the military and government officials. You'll fit well into ARC. There's only one formality left. You need to take a physical."

She'd been dreading this moment. "I can provide a document from my private doctor saying that I'm fit for duty."

"Tell me why you left the army, Gennie."

"I was a captain in Afghanistan, working with the Army Corps of Engineers. We were constructing a school in a remote village when we accidentally set off an explosive device." Though she'd told this story a hundred times, the words still triggered a rage deep inside. Her work crew had been betrayed. They never found out who was responsible for the bomb, but she blamed herself. She should have known better, should have made smarter decisions. Because she'd been careless, four friends had been killed in that explosion. And she would never stop being angry. "I was injured and evacuated."

Noah handed her a bottle of water from a mini-fridge beside the desk. "Do you know a former security contractor named Kenneth Warrick?"

"Yes." Hoping that he'd drop the subject, she took a long drink from the water bottle.

But Noah wasn't the sort of guy who gave up easily. "Tell me about him."

"A private contractor and weapons dealer, he was questioned regarding the explosion that killed my team. More than anyone else, he knew our schedule and our plans. I hate to think that he betrayed my crew."

"He wasn't charged."

And it wasn't the first time that Warrick smooth talked his way out of trouble. "The investigation concluded that a local warlord was responsible."

"You and Warrick were close."

So close that they'd discussed marriage. She would never allow herself to be that vulnerable again. "I was stupid."

He lowered himself into the chair beside the sofa. His gaze dropped, and he stared at her feet. Though she tried not to look down, she glanced. Her slacks were hiked up, and she could see her discolored ankle. The swollen flesh bulged over the top strap of her sandal.

"One of the guys downstairs is a medic," Noah said. "He could take a look at your injury."

"It's only a sprain."

"How do you know?"

She'd had enough broken bones to know when she had one. "I've been putting weight on my leg and it hasn't buckled. If I get the injury iced and wrapped with a bandage, I'll be fine."

"I have an assignment for you on Saturday," he said. "If you're not one hundred percent by then, I need to know."

"Yes, sir."

"Now, I want the rest of your story. Three years ago, you were injured in Afghanistan. According to the medical report, you had several broken bones and a concussion."

"That's correct."

"I don't need to know the medical procedures you've undergone, but I want the results. You have a disability."

Due to the concussion, damaged bones, a hematoma and extensive nerve damage, her left upper arm and certain muscles in both legs were numb. Ongoing programs of therapy and workouts had improved her condition. She passed her fitness tests with high marks, but there was one problem...not a problem, really, an anomaly.

She lifted her chin and confronted him directly. "In about thirty percent of my body, I can't feel pain."

Chapter Two

"Noah, are you sure it isn't too soon to have Gennie in the field?"

"I'm positive." He stared at the face on his cell phone's screen. Today, Anna Rose Claymore—the founder of ARC Security—wore her blue-streaked hair twisted in a bun atop her head. Her huge glasses had blue-and-pink-polka-dot frames. She looked several years too young to be the grandma of four—a phenomenon she attributed to being a full-fledged, dedicated nerd.

"Gennie Fox joined us only four days ago."

"You don't usually pay so much attention to field operations," he said. Anna Rose ran the cyber-crime division and generally stayed at her multiscreen array of computers. "What's up?"

"Gennie's condition fascinates me. She's like a comic book heroine whose superpower is being invulnerable to pain."

"And I'd advise you to never tell her that. She's not the type of woman who'd be complimented by a starring role in a comic."

"Ah, well, I guess that's *my* dream," Anna Rose said. "Is Gennie's sprain healed?"

"She's keeping her ankle wrapped, but our doctor gave her an okay for full activity. Yesterday, I saw her running on the treadmill without a limp. She's done well at every test we've come up with. Her marksmanship ranks at an expert level. She excels in hand-to-hand combat, and she understands our electronic equipment. Her greatest skill—one that can't be measured—is her ability to work well with the others on the team."

"Like I've said before, I approve of your decision to hire her. Gennie is remarkable and has contacts with people who might hire us."

He heard an unusual sour note in her voice. "What's troubling you?"

"It's not about Gennie." Above her glasses, her forehead scrunched with worry. "There's something off about this fund-raising event at General Haymarket's mansion. Why did he request a sweep of his house and grounds looking for explosives? He wants a metal scanner and ordered extra agents, including a sniper on the roof. Has our favorite general taken a deep dive into the paranoia pond?"

"I hope he's not losing it. He sends a lot of business our way."

"Send me a revised guest list," she said. "I'll check backgrounds and look for clues."

"Consider it done."

Noah ended the call and stepped back to watch as Gennie and other ARC field agents performed the pre-event security check at this palatial home southwest of Denver. The guest list that Anna Rose wanted would include the names of billionaires, high-ranking military personnel and influential executives. They'd allocated a good chunk of change for the privilege of attending this political event and were scheduled to start arriving in about an hour. During the silent auction, they'd drink artisan beer and whiskey from a local distillery. In keeping with the "Buy Colorado" theme, this elite group would chow down on stuffed mushrooms, venison, rattlesnake canapés and other regionally sourced delicacies arrayed on buffet tables.

Noah would have preferred a sit-down dinner where his team could easily keep an eye on the two hundred or so attendees. Instead, ARC needed to prepare for a roomful of Type-A personalities, accompanied by their equally aggressive spouses, all of whom would be competing in the auction, stating political views and matching wits. Even if there was no gunplay or exploding bombs, so much could go wrong.

For a moment, the red-and-gold glow of sunset flashed outside the west windows and distracted him. Beautiful and dangerous, the brilliant April skies were an omen that hinted at the onset of fire season. Instead of considering the potential for disaster, he focused on Gennie, noting her confident manner as she glided among the small circular tables in the center of the high-ceilinged, marble-floored ballroom. Her injured ankle didn't seem to bother her, and he figured she was wearing a compression wrap under her ankle-high boots that were low-heeled but classy. She looked like a million bucks in a form-hugging black jumpsuit and a patterned black-and-beige cashmere vest that was long enough to cover her holstered weapon.

She paused in her inspection of the tables. With a toss of her head that sent a ripple through her curly blond hair, she glanced over her shoulder and met his gaze. He nodded in her direction and reminded himself to keep a careful distance from this woman who was as beautiful as a Rocky Mountain sunset. *Another harbinger of danger!* Getting involved with an employee would be a seriously dumb decision, but there was no harm in scrutinizing her every move. That was his job.

From over his shoulder, he heard a gruff voice. "I never expected to see Captain Genevieve Fox in my home."

"General Haymarket." Noah shook hands with the vigorous older gentleman who was hosting this event. Haymarket was dressed in slacks and a striped golf shirt that stretched tightly across his barrel chest. He looked comfortable. The casual outfit suited him better than the dress uniform he'd be changing into before the event. Whether or not he was paranoid, this four-star general had paid his dues and put in his time. He was due for retirement.

"Did Gennie use me for a reference?" he asked.

"No, sir, she didn't."

"Are you aware that I have a history with her?"

She'd spoken to him about her complicated relationship with her former commanding officer. "I hope that's not a problem."

"Not on my end, but she's not real fond of me. The last time we spoke, she called me a bald-headed male chauvinist baboon. With all due respect, of course."

"Of course."

"I hate baboons." The general scowled. "She was mad because I wouldn't approve her return to active duty. After the bomb, she looked like hell. I couldn't allow her to put herself in harm's way, couldn't stand to see her hurt again."

"She's made a successful recovery," Noah said. *A remarkable woman.*

"You don't have a problem with her special condition?"

He didn't intend to say too much about Gennie's insensitivity to pain and her nerve damage. If she wanted to talk about her two years of operations, hard work and physical therapy with the general, that was her business. "The ARC doctor gave her a complete physical and rated her above average."

At the opposite end of the room, Gennie was paying particular attention to the floral arrangement beside the podium where the guest of honor, Mitch Murano, would be speaking. She leaned close to the thick green foliage, yellow flowers and dark red roses. Pulling back, she scowled at the posies as though they'd done something wrong. From there, she went to the silent auction tables where a variety of items were lined up side by side. Again, she inspected the flowers. She straightened her shoulders and made a beeline for him and the general.

The burly general who had commanded thousands of troops in Iraq and Afghanistan gave a shudder. "Do you think she's still angry?"

"You're not scared of her, are you, General?"

"Don't let those big blue eyes fool you. Pretty little Gennie is lethal. A few years ago, I saw her take down a trained combatant twice her size using only a broom handle for a weapon."

"I'm aware," Noah said. "Four days ago, she kicked my ass."

When she came to a halt in front of them, she raised her right hand so quickly that he thought for a moment that she was going to salute, even though the general wasn't in uniform and she was no longer a soldier. Or maybe she was going for a karate chop. Instead, she opted for a civilized handshake and a tentative smile.

"A pleasure to see you, sir."

"Likewise," he said. "Noah tells me that you're working for him."

"I am. And I have a security question about the floral displays. Should I speak to you about my concerns?"

"Not me. I don't know a damn thing about the decorations."

"Your wife?"

"Ruby didn't have anything to do with tonight. She's not even going to be here."

His wife's absence seemed odd to Noah. The spectacularly beautiful Ruby Haymarket usually grabbed any chance to break out the tiara and be the belle of the ball.

"I'll miss her," Gennie said. "I hope she's not ill."

"Fit as a fiddle and feisty, too. Her problem is that she doesn't share my political views. I believe Mitch Murano will make a damn fine senator. Ruby thinks he's a con man."

The general's wife had a point. In Noah's opinion, Murano had perfected the art of playing both sides against each other. While vigorously supporting gun rights, Murano ran a worldwide institute encouraging peaceful meditation and enlightenment. His detractors referred to his seesaw policies as NRA *Namaste*.

The general signaled to a man with a clipboard. "You

remember Captain Dean Slocum, don't you? He handled the food and decorations for this fund-raiser."

Slocum strutted toward them. His uniform was crisp. His grooming was perfect with his close-cropped pale blond hair as smooth as a platinum skull cap. He was so white that he was nearly albino. In the midst of bustling caterers and waiters making last minute preparations, Slocum appeared to be in control. He'd been the general's right-hand man for a long time and had grown smug in his job.

His sneering attitude wasn't the only reason Noah disliked the captain. After he shook Slocum's hand, he started to introduce Gennie.

"We're acquainted," she said coldly.

"I've known her for years." Slocum matched her coolness with an ice storm of his own. "Gennie's a hero and has the Purple Heart to prove it."

She flinched. Though she didn't feel pain in a third of her body, Noah could see that her memories of combat and working in a war zone still hurt. The nightmares and the guilt were harder to cure than physical impairments.

The general spoke to the captain. "Gennie has questions about the flowers, and I told her to ask you about them."

"No problem."

"I'll leave you to it. Gennie, I hope we can talk later." He backed out of the conversation. "Right now, I'd better run upstairs and get changed."

"Give Ruby my regards," she said with a smile that faded as she turned back to Slocum. "When you ordered the arrangements, did you specify colors or types of flowers?"

"No." With the general gone, Slocum didn't bother to hide his hostility. His blue eyes narrowed to slits in his colorless face. "I told them that the flowers were for a fund-raiser and gave them the size and number of the arrangements. When I mentioned Mitch Murano, the flower people were thrilled. He's a celebrity. I hope he brings his supermodel girlfriend. Have you ever seen her?"

"I don't know who she is or what she looks like," Gennie said.

"Of course not. It's obvious that you aren't interested in fashion. My question is, why the hell are you making trouble?"

"About the flowers," she said, "you didn't request yellow oleander, pink rhododendron and hemlock branches. Is that correct?"

"I already said I didn't." He flipped through his clipboard, made a note and tore off a scrap of paper, which he tossed to her. "This is the florist. If you need more details, call them."

"I will." She pulled out her cell phone and stepped aside.

Slocum pivoted on his heel so he was facing toward Noah again. "You need to keep your people in line, and I'm not just talking about Gennie. I have a problem with your man at the front entrance."

Shrugging off his irritation with Slocum's tone, Noah remained professional. "Which man at the entrance?"

"The pretty boy, he said his name was Tony Vega and claimed that his orders were to set up a metal detector. That's a waste of time. Some of the people coming to this event are military and could be in full dress uniform, possibly including sabers. Others are ranchers who routinely carry guns. These are rich men, powerful men, and they won't give a damn if they set off a beeper. No way will they surrender their weapons."

Providing security for people who refused to disarm made Noah's job more difficult, but he wasn't responsible for this particular scan. "Talk to the general about disarming his guests. He specifically asked for the metal detector."

"And I'm telling you to take it down."

Seriously? This pencil-neck geek thought he could overrule the general? "I won't do it without written authorization to change the terms of our contract."

"Fine." He flipped to a blank page on his clipboard and started writing.

"What's the deal with this event?" In normal circumstances, Noah would have covered this fund-raiser with five or six operatives, but the general requested twelve, including outdoor surveillance. "Is there something we need to be aware of? Have you received threats?"

"Not your problem, Noah."

The hell it wasn't. Managing the danger level was the very definition of protective security. "I'll take this up with the general."

"Wait!" Slocum caught his arm before he could leave. "Several people—including a blond anchor on TV—are mad at Murano. He's had a dozen or so threats from people who are unhappy with those screwball meditation classes he teaches."

"And?"

"The threats were neutralized."

Noah didn't like the sound of that. Slocum was talking like an evil James Bond villain. "Neutralized how?"

"His people took care of it. Talk to them."

The entourage for Mitch Murano included bodyguards and advisors. "How many of them are there?"

"Don't know. Don't care." Slocum tore the sheet of paper off his clipboard. "This note instructs you to take down the metal detectors. I signed it, dated it and will take responsibility."

"I intend to inform the general of the change in contract."

"You do that." He pivoted and made a quick exit.

Gladly, Noah returned to Gennie. He didn't understand her problem with the flowers, but when she had mentioned hemlock, it caught his attention.

She ended her phone call and frowned at him. "You didn't tell me everything about this assignment."

His patience was running thin after the snippy conversation with Slocum, and he didn't like her insinuation that he was somehow trying to trick her. "You know everything you need to know."

"I wasn't aware that information was on a need-to-know basis."

He was *not* going to get into an argument. The guests would be arriving soon. "Tell me what you learned from the florist."

"The flowers used in these arrangements include yellow oleander, pink rhododendron, white azaleas, sprigs of hemlock and roses that are such a dark red that they appear to be black. Does that suggest anything to you?"

Though he could see that she was fighting to keep her anger under control, her flushed cheeks and clenched jaw betrayed the hostility raging just below the surface. And he was feeling much the same. "I don't get it."

"Even if you don't know anything about the language of flowers—which clearly you do not—I'd expect you to recognize common poisons. If you had to survive in nature, what would you eat?"

"I could do without the sarcasm."

"All these plants are toxic, except for the roses, and black roses symbolize death."

His gaze darted around the room, noticing the large display at the podium and six smaller versions on surrounding tables. "How dangerous are they?"

"There's no problem unless the guests start eating the flowers or rubbing them on their bodies. I'm surprised that the florist agreed to handle these plants."

She crossed the marble floor to one of the tables with a tall spreading display of flowers, and he followed. "They don't look dangerous."

"Anyone who knows about plants will recognize the threat. They're a warning. And that's why I talked to the florist about why they used these flowers. They said they were fulfilling a request, and here's where this story gets interesting."

"How so?"

She plucked one of the dark velvety roses from the display. "Guess who made the request for all these poisonous flowers?"

He didn't have time to play games. "Tell me."

"The name the florist gave me was… Kenneth Warrick."

Chapter Three

Gennie was good at reading people, not that it took any particular sensitivity to deduce that Noah was furious. His brow furrowed like a grumpy—but still handsome—troll, and she could almost see steam shooting out of his ears, which was pretty much the reaction she'd expected. If there was one thing she'd learned about her boss during the past four days, it was that he hated when any situation got out of his control.

Though equally outraged, Gennie tamped down her anger. She twirled the dark rose between her fingers. "Did Warrick send these flowers as a warning? Or as a threat?"

"Hell if I know."

His dark brown eyes returned her gaze with an intensity that made her feel like he was peering inside her skull. *Looking for what?* She had no hidden agenda. Her attitude toward Warrick was unambiguous hatred. As far as she was concerned, Noah was the wild card. He had mentioned Warrick at their first meeting, but he didn't give context. Were they connected? Was Warrick a friend or an enemy? A muscle in Noah's jaw twitched, but he said nothing. *If that was the way he wanted to play it, fine.*

She squared off with him and went silent.

They were both stubborn enough to continue this stare down for a very long time. She took the opportunity to study his face, which was definitely masculine in spite of the dimples that tweaked the corners of his mouth when he grinned. He was saved from being too classically handsome by his square jaw, sharp cheekbones and the tension that deepened the wrinkles on his forehead and around his eyes. She wondered what he'd look like with longer hair and maybe a beard.

Speculation on Noah's grooming was none of her business. Whether he shaved or not, she didn't give a hoot. Gennie had never been the type of giggly girl who got all jacked up over a good-looking male. She needed to figure out why Warrick requested those flowers. *Warning or threat, which was it?*

She cleared her throat. "Is Kenneth Warrick coming to this event?"

"He's not on the guest list."

"That's not what I asked."

"I have no reason to expect he'll be here."

"In our first interview, you mentioned Warrick. Is he an associate of yours?"

"Hell, no."

Could she trust Noah? If she was going to work with him, she had to know that he had her back. "How did you meet Warrick?"

"We've never come face-to-face."

She could tell that he was rationing his words but had no idea why. They were on the same team, weren't they? Motioning for him to walk beside her, she strolled across the marble floor of the ballroom toward the kitchen where the caterers and the waitstaff bustled. Some carried trays of canapés. Others made final preparations by slicing, dicing and arranging. Two hours ago when she'd arrived at this massive three-story red brick Colonial house with six pillars across the front, she'd been excited about her assignment and anxious to do a good job—similar to how she used to feel with her team of army engineers. In Afghanistan, she'd been aware of the ever-present danger, but she hadn't been fearful. And she wasn't scared now, just apprehensive. She'd peeked under a stone and uncovered a scorpion.

She stopped a caterer in a chef's jacket and asked him to clip the stem on her rose. Using his knife, he did so and handed the bloom back to her with a flourish. She rewarded him with a smile, passed on a bit of advice about steering clear of the poisonous flowers in the arrangements and then turned back to Noah. "I know Warrick is acquainted with the general."

"He's on a list of people to watch for. That's why I mentioned him to you. By the way, Slocum hates him."

She scanned the room until she spotted the overly tidy blond captain with his clipboard. "He hates everybody."

"You have issues with Slocum?"

"Maybe." She glimpsed a slight reaction from Noah, a narrowing of his eyes and a twitch of his mouth. "Do you have your own grudge against Slocum?"

"First, you tell me."

While she'd been recovering from her injuries, Haymarket had offered her a job as his aide, taking over many of Slocum's duties. Though she'd turned down the position, the captain was her sworn enemy for life. She didn't really want to talk about it. "Let's just say that he doesn't like me."

"Is there anybody in the military you haven't pissed off?"

"Maybe not." Though she remained curious about his beef with Slocum, she let it go. "Will you inform the general about the flowers?"

"Yes, and I'll also ask about Warrick." He frowned. "I think Haymarket is expecting trouble. Why else would he ask for a metal scanner and extra security outside the house?"

She'd wondered the same thing. The sniper on the roof seemed way too excessive for a fancy political fund-raiser. "He didn't explain to you?"

"He did not."

"Typical," she said. "He plays his cards close to the vest."

"Sounds like you know him better than I do."

Her friendship with General Haymarket developed during her first tour of duty in faraway Afghanistan after he'd discovered that she grew up in his home state of Colorado. They'd known some of the same people, skied at the same resorts and fished in the same creeks. After her injury, he'd been too protective, but she never doubted that he had her best interests at heart. When Noah told her about this assignment, she'd been looking forward to seeing her former commanding officer. Someday, she hoped they could mend fences.

Friendship with the general was a mostly good memory from her military service. Kenneth Warrick was the opposite. The only way she wanted to see him was through the crosshairs of a rifle scope. After she'd been discharged from the hospital—where he never once visited—she'd done her best to erase him from her mind. Through the grapevine, she'd heard that his legitimate business as a private contractor and weapons dealer had taken a nefarious turn, and he'd dropped off the grid.

"Warrick used his real name when he talked to the florist." She looked up at Noah. "I had the impression that he didn't want to advertise his whereabouts."

"Could be trying to tell us something," Noah said. "Is he aware of your knowledge of plants and flowers?"

"I'm sure he is. One time, he gave me a bouquet of irises as a symbol for intelligence and courage. Quite a compliment." At that point in their relationship, she would have preferred brilliant red roses meaning passionate love, but there were worse things than being smart and brave. "Why do you ask?"

"The poisonous flowers are a warning that most people wouldn't understand. But he knew you would. He might have used his name to attract your attention."

She shuddered at the idea of Warrick sending her a message. "If he wanted to contact me, I'm not hard to find. He could pick up the phone and call. Or drop by the house."

"Does he have your address?"

"It's not hard to figure out." She lived in her parents' house in north Denver. They'd made a permanent move to Phoenix and were glad to have her taking care of the place. "We're getting off track. Our main concern is security for this event."

Wryly, he said, "I'm the boss. That's supposed to be my line."

"It shows we're on the same page." And she was proud of herself for not straying off track. When Noah flashed one of his infrequent grins and hiked up his right eyebrow in a question mark, he could be incredibly distracting. She squashed a crazy urge to trace the line of his lips with the nearly black rose. Instead, she tucked the flower behind her ear.

To her surprise, he reached up and brushed his fingers through her hair. "You make me think of *Carmen*. It's pretty."

"But not practical." She wanted to look like a security guard not an opera singer or tango dancer. She removed the flower and slipped it into the pocket of his gray sports jacket.

"Here's a thought," Noah said. "The threat might be aimed at Mitch Murano."

Apart from a general outline of Murano's accomplishments, her only information came from one of the other ARC employees. Gennie looked across the dining hall toward the redhead with the great physique. "Zoey Potter took a three-week course with Murano. She said he turned her life around."

Noah checked his G-SHOCK wristwatch. "The guests will be here soon. In light of Warrick's involvement, I'd understand if you wanted to take the rest of the day off."

"Not a chance."

"Very well," he said. "Talk to Zoey and see if there's a link between Murano and Warrick."

She stifled the instinct to salute. "Thanks for trusting me."

His grin blossomed again. "Trust goes both ways."

"Yes, it does."

She watched him walk away. Though he hadn't set out to be disarming, he couldn't help the charm that radiated from him. In a few short minutes, she'd gone from anxious and irritated to nearly trusting the man. She wanted to believe that Noah was one of the good guys. He'd taken a chance by hiring her, and she didn't intend to let him down no matter what kind of trouble Warrick was brewing.

NOAH STRODE ACROSS the polished floor in the impressive entryway to General Haymarket's mansion. A crystal chandelier shimmered overhead, the side tables were polished antiques from an era he couldn't name, but he knew the sculptures resting upon them were original Remington cowboys. Noah thought of the foyer as an example of the general's rugged outlook mixed with Ruby's taste for sparkle. Haymarket was the sort of man who braved the wilderness to pan for gold, and she was the lady who made his nuggets into a necklace. Despite their age difference—he was in his sixties and she in her forties—they seemed happy. In a weird way, they complemented each other.

Noah paused to issue a quick instruction to Tony Vega, telling him to hold off on the metal detector. Then he ascended the curving staircase, taking two steps at a time, hoping that a talk with the general would clear up his questions about Warrick.

Outside the general's bedroom, he came to a halt with

his fist raised to knock. From inside, he heard an argument. General Haymarket's voice was gruff and mono-
syllabic. The woman sounded like a soprano singing an
aria. It had to be Ruby. She'd already made it clear that
she didn't like this fund-raiser, and now she was telling
him that she had no intention of making an appearance.

Noah's unfortunate marriage had ended in divorce
five years ago, and he had plenty of experience with
domestic tirades—enough that he knew better than to
interrupt. Stepping back, he leaned against the wall
in the wide hallway and put through another call to
Anna Rose. Her face popped up on the screen of his
cell phone.

With her index finger, she pushed her polka-dot
glasses up on her nose and said, "There's a suspicious
person working as a security agent for Mitch Murano."

"Why suspicious?"

"A series of cyber indicators lead me to believe that
he's using a fake identity."

As she rattled off an impressive number of clues
that led to her conclusion, he tried not to eavesdrop on
the general and Ruby. The word *liar* was being ban-
died about, also *cheating*, *scum-sucking creep*. On both
sides, it was harsh.

He stepped away from the door. "Anna Rose, I think
you're onto something."

"Thank you, dear. There are times when this old
computer broad hits the mark. Call me Super Cyber
Anna Banana."

"Another comic book character?"

"Actually, it's what my grandson Flip calls me. Anna

Banana is sparkly and does shape-shifting, usually turning into fruit."

"In the meantime…"

"I ran facial recognition on this guy and came up with a match."

"Kenneth Warrick?"

"Bingo!"

Gennie's former boyfriend was becoming a problem. "Send me his most recent photo and I'll alert everybody to be on the lookout."

"I'll dig into links between Warrick and Murano and the general," she said.

"Add Ruby Haymarket into that mix. She took a class with Murano."

As if responding to a cue, Ruby charged into the hallway, leaving the bedroom door open behind her. Over her shoulder, she shouted at the general, "Don't try to stop me. I can't stand Mitch Murano, and I refuse to pretend that I like the man."

The half-dressed general followed her through the door. "You won't be missed. I'll be too busy chatting up Lydia Green and Crystal."

"Seriously, Roger? Are you trying to make me jealous?" Her honey-blond hair was caught up in a high ponytail that fell past the collar of her shirt. Her sculpted eyebrows arched in disdain. "You can talk to those piglets all you want. I'm going for a ride."

Noah stood directly in her path. Stepping out of the way wasn't in his nature, and so he squared his shoulders and stood his ground. "Good afternoon, ma'am."

"I'm not old enough to be a *ma'am*. We're probably the same age."

Give or take a decade. "Did I hear you say that you were going for a ride?"

"That's right." She braced her fists on the hips of her skinny jeans and glared at him. "Have you got a problem with that?"

"It's none of my business unless your ride puts you in harm's way. I want to be certain that you're safe. Allow me to escort you."

He cocked his arm, and she latched on. "If you want to ride with me, I have a stallion you might be able to handle."

"I'm needed here, but I'll instruct one of my men to take you to the stables."

She tossed a glance over her shoulder at her husband. "Don't wait up for me."

"I won't." The general's face was blistering red. "I don't give a hot damn if you settle your cute little behind into the saddle and ride across the mountains to California. It might jostle some sense into that pea brain of yours."

"He doesn't get me," she whispered to Noah, "and he never will. Not until the day he dies."

He sincerely hoped that day didn't come on his watch.

Chapter Four

The small circular tables scattered in the center of the ballroom were meant for standing and chatting while sampling from the buffet. Before the guests arrived, they were vacant. Gennie wended her way through the tables and across the dance floor to approach Zoey. Though the redhead wore a modest pantsuit with sleeves that covered her ripped biceps, she still looked buff. Not an ounce of flab on that tanned well-toned body.

She greeted Gennie. "So, G-Fox, are you ready for this party to get started?"

"I've got one question. How much do you know about flowers?"

Zoey smiled and shrugged. "They smell good?"

After a quick lecture on the toxic posies in the floral displays, Gennie mentioned Kenneth Warrick. "Have you heard of him? He used to be a private contractor in Afghanistan."

"I was in the navy, never stationed in the Middle East."

"He placed the order with the florist requesting those particular flowers, maybe as a threat to the guest of honor. What can you tell me about Murano?"

Zoey kept her eyes straight ahead and spoke out of the corner of her mouth as if dribbling out a secret. "I wouldn't be surprised if this Warrick character wanted to poison Murano. Lots of people have a beef with him...including me."

"Wait a minute!" Gennie was unsure she'd heard correctly. "You said Murano changed your life."

"That doesn't mean I like the guy. He claims to be spiritual and says his method is *tough love*, but there was nothing lovely about the way he treated me. After I left the navy, I was in a real bad place. My weight dropped to ninety-eight pounds. I dosed my morning orange juice with vodka, and that was when I bothered to get up. Mostly I stayed in bed and stayed stoned."

"Weed?"

"And worse. I can't believe I abused my body like that." Her side-talking lips pinched together. "I hit rock bottom. That's where smarmy Mitch Murano and his promise of meditation and healing came into play. I dropped four grand on a course with him. His idea of treatment was to tell me in no uncertain terms that I was hopeless and would never amount to anything. After a few weeks with him, I wanted to die."

Gennie listened without comment. She empathized and identified with the emotional struggle that often came when leaving the service. Her injuries and the deaths of her team fed her PTSD. There had been days when she'd stared into the abyss and longed for death.

"Then I got angry," Zoey said.

"I understand."

"I was determined to prove my worth. Started working out like a woman possessed. I took martial arts classes and boxing, spent hours with the heavy bag, picturing Murano's face and punching hard. After gallons of sweat and tears, I discovered the skills and talent for honing my body. I got strong. Nobody was ever going to hurt me again."

"Do you think Murano meant for that to happen?" Gennie suggested. "Maybe he planned it that way."

"I considered the possibility, but when I tried to thank him, Murano didn't even remember my name. All he wanted was to sell me another class."

She looked toward the ballroom entrance, and Gennie followed her gaze. Three other field agents—two black and one white, all former Army Rangers—had their heads together. She knew that they were armed, skilled combatants. With all this security, she shouldn't have felt apprehensive in the least. Her gaze went toward the poisonous flowers. *Warning or threat?* "How did Murano connect with the general?"

"His wife took classes with the guru, and she ended up hating him like I do. You'd think that the general would stand up for Ruby. But that didn't happen. He talked to Murano, and they hit it off, literally. They're golf buddies."

Her phone and Zoey's rang at the same time. Noah had sent a text to the entire ARC team, telling them to be on the lookout for Kenneth Warrick. If sighted, they should detain him. Gennie's screen filled with a photograph of the man she'd once loved.

"He's cute," Zoey said.

"Not my type." She noticed the tiny scar bisecting his left eyebrow, the only injury he'd sustained in the explosion that changed her life forever.

Zoey reached into her jacket pocket and took out an electronic earpiece. "Have you ever used one of these?"

"Nothing as sophisticated as this, but I understand how it works." She adjusted the volume and placed the device into her ear before attaching a mic to the collar of her jumpsuit. "It's weird having people talk inside my head."

Zoey whispered into her microphone, "Any questions?"

"I'm good for now."

"Okay, G-Fox. It's time for you to move into position."

"Copy that."

With a nod, she moved to the quadrant of the ballroom that she was supposed to be watching. Because she was the newest member of the team, she was stationed toward the rear at the farthest point away from the riser and podium where a small jazz band was setting up. To her right were the windows that showcased a brilliant Rocky Mountain sunset. The wall to her left held portraits in elaborate frames, including one of Ruby on horseback. Too bad she wasn't here! Gennie would have liked to hear her opinions about Murano. In spite of what Zoey had said, the guru couldn't be a total jerkwad. After all, the general liked him enough to host this grand fund-raiser.

She glanced across the ballroom toward where Zoey was standing at the edge of a wide corridor with glass French doors that stood open. The powder rooms, an office and a library were in that direction. A couple of hours ago when Gennie had been scanning for explosives, bugs and other potential problems, she'd explored and fallen in love with the spacious library that had bookcases on every wall and comfortable overstuffed furniture for curling up and reading. The tall arched windows offered a charming view of the stable and attached corral. After this event was over, she might be able to spend some time in that library with the general, and they could reconnect.

Until then, she was on duty.

And the guests were arriving.

This type of high-class security while not in uniform was new to her, and she enjoyed exercising her powers of observation. While she watched and listened, the room gradually filled with polished gentlemen and well-dressed women. If half their jewels were the real thing, the Haymarket mansion would have been a bonanza for a thief. She caught a hint of gossip, mostly suggestions that the general was having an affair. The fact that Ruby had skipped this event fanned those flames.

Tony Vega's voice came through the earpiece. "Heads up, everybody. The guru is here."

While continuing to keep an eye on the people in her quadrant, Gennie circled around the outer tables where people were seated and surveyed the central array where others stood and drank and talked. Though many of the guests had arrived, the large ballroom wasn't crowded. Curious, she took a position where she could get a peek at Murano. Others flocked around him, moths to a flame. In the midst of that adoring group, she glimpsed his shoulder-length black hair, heavy brows and toothy smile. He was shorter than she'd expected, probably only five foot ten. But there was something that made him seem large. His fan club would have called it charisma, but she sensed an over-inflated ego that puffed him up like a balloon. His trademark was a glittering circular brooch he wore at his throat as a bolo tie—an example of the famous Murano glass that was manufactured by his ancestors in Italy.

She spied Noah as he moved toward her. *Now, there was a man who didn't need sparkles to stand out!* Her boss did nothing to attract attention, but she couldn't look away. His stride showed a natural athleticism. Maybe she was imagining things, but it seemed like other people cleared a path for him. Gennie wasn't the only one watching Noah. The bejeweled ladies took notice. And when he came to a halt beside her, she felt a little bit special.

"Have you seen your old buddy from Afghanistan?" he asked.

"He's not my bud. And no, I have not." When she looked back toward Murano, he seemed to be watching her...or not. Why would he be interested in her? "What else have you learned about Warrick?"

"He's been working security for Murano under an alias."

"That's a scoop. How did you find out?"

"Anna Rose, our boss and resident cyber genius, tracked him down on her computer. I asked the head of Murano's security about Warrick, using his alias. He's not on the schedule for today."

"How many guests?" she asked.

"Three hundred fifteen, including spouses."

"And how many security people does Murano have with him?"

"Today, it's three."

ARC had twelve, including the guy on the roof,

and Murano had three. Fifteen trained security agents to handle a couple hundred people at a fund-raiser in Denver seemed way over the top. The atmosphere felt forced, like the jazz band playing upbeat tunes. No blues for Mitch Murano. "What kind of event is this? When I worked security for the US Embassy in Kabul, we had fewer guards."

"It's what the general wanted. Not the way I would have handled things, but I'm not paying the bill."

"Did you set up the metal detector?"

"Upon consideration, the general agreed with Slocum that his guests would be insulted by us asking them to disarm."

"Wouldn't want to upset the donors." She felt like they were in a war zone.

"When I mentioned Warrick to the general, he denied having contact with him."

Though she really wanted to be friends with the general again, she didn't altogether believe his denial. "Wasn't he the one who warned us about Warrick?"

"The instruction actually came from Slocum."

"But the general must know that Warrick works for Murano. They golf together. Wouldn't the general have run into him?"

"I'm not going to push. Figuring out the undercurrents isn't our job."

The hell it wasn't. "With all due respect, Noah, you're dead wrong. Security is about more than reacting to an overt threat. We need to be able to decipher the undercurrents and anticipate the enemy's next move."

She held her breath, watching him and waiting for his response. The minute she'd opened her mouth, she knew that she was being seriously insubordinate. Noah would be justified if he fired her on the spot.

"With all due respect?" He grinned. "You've got a real talent for making enemies."

"So I've been told."

"But I'm not going to line up against you, Gennie. I hate to admit when I'm dead wrong. So, I'll just say that you're right about figuring out what the hell is going on here. We need to know. In the meantime, we'll watch over the valuables and try to keep these people from killing each other."

"Yes, sir."

A tall man in a rear admiral's uniform waved to Noah. "I've got to meet and greet some of our past and future clients. If you see Warrick, use your mic and let us know. Hang in there, Gennie. You're doing a good job."

"Copy that."

She restrained an urge to hug him or follow him across the room like a besotted puppy dog. Of the many officers and supervisors she'd worked under, very few would admit a mistake. Noah was a good leader. He made her feel valued, as though her insights mattered.

Milling around and trying to be invisible, she observed as the guests munched on native Colorado foods, including the infamous Rocky Mountain oysters, and drank Colorado brews and placed their bids on silent auction items. She'd spotted a rancher in a Western-style suit with a holster clipped to his belt and a sweet-faced lady who revealed her Colt .45 when she opened her needlepoint satchel to take out a hanky. In spite of the artillery, neither seemed prone to violence.

The crowd swelled as the band switched to a couple of John Denver songs designed for singing along. As the guests chanted "Rocky Mountain High"—officially designated as the second state song—she heard Tony Vega through her earpiece. "I need backup at the entrance to handle a couple of drunks."

"I'm on my way," Zoey responded. "G-Fox, you need to cover my area, as well as yours."

She turned on her microphone with a touch. "I'm on it."

The corridor where Zoey had been standing was a lot busier than Gennie's area because the restrooms were down that hall. Trying to avoid looking like a bathroom monitor, she paced behind the silent auction tables where well-displayed photos showed the vacation trips, jewelry, electronics and other goodies.

Outside, the sunset was turning to dusk. Several small crystal chandeliers glimmered and artful, indirect lighting spread a flattering glow throughout the ballroom. Gennie wished the lights were brighter so she could see clearly.

After a few minutes, Tony's voice came through the earpiece again. "All clear."

Gennie wasn't so sure. She didn't feel like they were in the clear. Something was off. Though the air was still, a sudden chill sent goose bumps up and down her arms.

Then she saw him.

Kenneth Warrick turned away from her and sauntered toward the corridor that led to the restrooms. Though she'd only had a quick glance, she could tell that he'd altered his appearance by changing his hair, covering the scar in his eyebrow and growing a beard.

He didn't look much like the photo Noah had sent to the team, but she knew him. Gennie would never forget the set of his shoulders and the cocky way he walked. He paused at the open French doors outside the corridor, turned his head and made direct eye contact. Then he blew her a kiss.

Bastard! She activated her mic. "I need backup. Kenneth Warrick is in the hall outside the bathrooms."

Leaving the auction tables, she took her Beretta from the holster and held it close to her side to avoid frightening the guests. At the entrance to the corridor, she glimpsed the door to the library closing.

Before she could follow, a man grasped her left arm. She didn't feel pain but the pressure alerted her to a strong grip. Acting on pure instinct, she broke free and whirled. Before she retaliated with a blow to his throat, gut and crotch, she stopped herself. "Mr. Murano," she said.

"Actually, it's Dr. Murano, but I don't like to stand on ceremony. Please call me Mitch." He treated her to a close-up view of his twinkly white smile and the glittering fastener on his bolo tie. "You're Gennie Fox, aren't you? The general told me about you."

"Excuse me, sir."

"Surely, you can spare a few minutes. I'm fascinated by your insensitivity to pain. Does it affect the dexterity in your hands?"

There was no polite way to end this conversation. "I can't talk now."

With a pivot, she dashed down the corridor toward the closed library door. She was pleased to see that Zoey and one of the other guys had responded to her call for backup and joined her. To her chagrin, Murano was close behind them. *Where the hell is Noah?* Gennie wanted him to be there when she met Warrick. No time to wait.

She tried the handle on the door. Of course, it was locked. She was reminded of when she had to break into the mountain cabin to rescue the fake hostage. Dropping to her knees, she picked the lock in seconds.

Behind her, she heard Zoey talking into her mic. "We need backup at the library."

Gennie pushed the door open and raised her Beretta in both hands. The lights were on, illuminating the horror. She saw blood, so much blood. And then…

"Noah!"

He was exiting the library through a tall open window. His bloody handprint smeared the glass.

Chapter Five

The killer was getting away. Noah stumbled through the hinged library window onto the lawn, staggered to his feet and tried to focus his blurred vision. The last rays of sunset were fading into dusk, making the world indistinct. In the distance, he saw the killer escaping, riding a chestnut horse toward the stable. Noah had to stop him.

He remembered the sniper on the roof. Hoping to alert the shooter, he reached for his microphone. Gone! He'd lost his mic and earbud. His gun had been taken and his cell phone. *What the hell happened?* He'd gotten a call from Slocum asking him to meet in the library. Noah remembered opening the library door, wondering why no one had turned on the overhead lights, and then…

His memory returned in flashes. Zapped by a stun gun, he fell to the floor, writhing. High voltage shock tore through his body. Every cell screamed in pain. Darkness consumed him. After a moment of unconsciousness, his eyelids pried open. The room was lit. He saw Slocum sprawled on the sofa with his pale blue eyes wide open and staring at the ceiling. A chest wound desecrated his uniform. The captain must have struggled because his blood was spattered and smeared everywhere. His throat had been slashed.

Noah had tried to help him, to put pressure on the carotid. He'd been too late. Dean Slocum was already dead. *And the killer was getting away.*

"Noah, what are you doing?"

Looking over his shoulder, he saw Gennie climbing through the window. Good, he needed her help... and her cell phone. He stuck out his hand. "Give me your phone."

"What happened to your phone?"

He didn't have time to explain. "Your mic, give me your mic."

"Or you could tell me who I should talk to and what I should say."

Stubborn woman! But he was too groggy to argue, and daylight was almost gone. "Tell Tony I need his bike."

She gently touched his arm. "Please tell me what happened."

"I'm still in charge, and I need a motorcycle. Now!"

"Yes, sir."

Verifying that she was doing as he'd ordered, he tried to gain his equilibrium while struggling against a whirlpool of vertigo. His knees threatened to buckle. If he didn't get moving, he'd go unconscious again. He set out toward the horse barn in a lurching, clumsy gait. The shock from the stun gun shouldn't have had this sort of effect. While he was unconscious, he must have been drugged.

Gennie stepped up beside him. "We should wait for Tony."

"No time." He pointed toward the stables. "The killer went this way. On horseback."

"Did you see him commit the murder?"

"I was unconscious, hit by a stun gun, maybe drugged." When he shook his head, the inside of his skull rattled and throbbed. "I tried to help him but couldn't find a pulse."

"If you're so damned determined to walk, you might as well hang on to me." She draped his arm over her shoulder to give support. "Can you identify the killer?"

"The window was open." A memory slipped through his mind like a shadow in the wind. "After I knew Slocum was dead, I went to the window. I saw him mount the horse."

"Do you remember what he was wearing? Or his hair color? Anything?"

"Not enough light. It was too vague."

"You'll remember," she said.

His movements were still awkward, but his mind had begun to clear. Even if he and Gennie didn't catch up to the man fleeing on horseback, there were surveillance cameras at the general's mansion and Morris, the Marine-trained sharpshooter on the roof. "Morris might have seen the killer."

Tony rode around the corner of the house on his lightweight two-rider Yamaha. Avoiding the new grass, he parked on a pathway, jumped off the bike and rushed toward them. "Are you okay, Noah?"

"I've been better. What the hell are you wearing?"

"Sorry about the sweatshirt," Tony mumbled. "I was handling a drunk, the situation got gross and I had to change."

Later, they'd laugh. "You need to contact the police, shut down the library crime scene and don't let anyone leave the grounds."

"Got it." Tony knew what to do. In most circumstances, he was second-in-command on field assignments.

"Also, contact Morris on the roof. Find out if he was in position to see anyone leave the library."

"What are you going to do?"

"I'm going to catch this guy."

Gennie opened the trunk on the Yamaha, took out a rag and tossed it to him. "You need to clean up. We're going to ride together, and I don't want to get blood all over this jumpsuit."

He rubbed at the blood in the creases of his hand and dabbed the smears on the cuff of his white shirt and his jacket sleeve. Too much blood! He tore off his jacket and threw it on the ground, then rolled his sleeves up to his elbow. "How's this?"

"Not bad," she said.

He wondered when the balance of power between them had changed. Somehow, Gennie had stepped up and taken charge.

She mounted the bike and put on her helmet. "I'll drive. You're in no condition."

Though he agreed, he still felt like a weenie when he climbed onto the back. The helmet Tony gave his usually female companions was purple and sparkly. Noah stuck it onto his head. Could have been worse; could have been painted with twinkle stars and unicorns.

She started the engine, turned on the headlight and glanced back toward him. "Hang on."

Oddly, he hadn't considered the possibility that she wouldn't know how to handle a motorcycle. Gennie was the type of woman who could do anything from building a school in Afghanistan to besting him in a physical encounter. Some men would have been threatened by her competence. Not Noah. How could he be ashamed about sitting behind her on the bike when it felt so good to lean against her? He wrapped his arms around her slender waist as she drove.

As they neared the stable, he tapped her shoulder. "Stop here."

He wanted to find out if the horse had been taken from the barn or had come from a neighbor's house. Though he probably wouldn't recognize the getaway animal, he could tell if the horses in the barn had recently been ridden. They could arrange for a horsey lineup. Imagining that scene, he chuckled. *What's wrong with me?* He'd been attacked and witnessed a brutal murder. *Nothing funny about that!* Maybe the drug he'd been given was a variation on laughing gas.

Gennie applied the brake, parked, dismounted and drew her gun. After taking off her helmet, she approached the barn. Since his weapon was gone, he had no choice but to follow.

In the distance, a police siren screamed. Gennie paused and looked over her shoulder. "I can't believe this is happening."

"When you work for ARC, you've got to be ready for anything."

She glared through the dusk. "Do you have a lot of cold-blooded murders on your security assignments?"

"If we did, we'd lose customers." Again, he felt a

grin creep across his face. Definitely not funny! Slo-cum's murder would discourage other clients. "We need to catch this guy."

"Because it's bad for business?" She shook her head and scowled. "Let's get on with it. Where's your gun?"

"It was taken, along with my earpiece and micro-phone."

She handed over her Beretta. Hiking up the pant leg of her jumpsuit, she took a second gun from an ankle hol-ster. Weapons at the ready, they entered the horse barn. There didn't appear to be anybody inside, which kind of surprised him. Noah would have expected Ruby to assign one of her employees to watch over her precious horses while there were so many strangers in the house.

"Hello," he called out. "Anybody here?"

Gennie flicked the light switch inside the wide barn door. There were three stalls on the right side and four on the left, but only two were occupied. The horses pranced and nickered, agitated. Maybe they didn't like the sirens that had grown louder as the police and am-bulance came closer. He searched the areas where feed and tackle were stored. Still, he found no one.

"Ruby came out here earlier," he said. "She wanted to go for a ride."

"Do you think she's working with the killer?"

The thought hadn't occurred to him. He shook his head, hoping to jump-start his brain. If he wanted to figure out what happened, he needed to get a lot smarter a lot faster. "Why would you suspect her?"

"Circumstance," Gennie said. "You saw a man on horseback, and Ruby was out here with the horses. I don't think she had much of a motive. Slocum annoyed her, but he annoyed everybody. If being an officious jerk was a valid reason to commit murder, the morgue would be filled with bureaucrats."

With a steadier stride, he left the barn. "I didn't see Ruby at the party."

"If she wanted Slocum dead, she could have hired someone to do it and provided them with a horse to make their escape."

He returned to the Yamaha and claimed the black helmet for himself, leaving the sparkly purple for her. "We'll take this trail behind the barn. Try to reach higher ground where we can look for the man on horseback."

"In the dark?"

"The moon's coming up. We can't quit now."

Her grip on the chrome handlebars showed confidence, but her voice was nervous. "I'm pretty sure that I know who killed Slocum."

Another memory flashed in his mind. He heard her voice inside his head. "You saw Kenneth Warrick."

Avoiding his gaze, she nodded. "He blew me a kiss."

"Are you certain it was him?"

"One hundred percent." Her jaw tensed. "He looks different, changed his hair color and grew a beard. But I knew it was him. He was entering the wide corridor outside the library. If I'd been faster, I could have stopped him."

It wasn't her fault. There was plenty of guilt to go around.

GENNIE GOT ON the motorcycle and revved the engine. Chasing across the countryside in search of someone like Warrick—a clever planner who had undoubtedly determined the best escape route—was futile. Still, there wasn't much else they could do.

"Security cameras," Noah said as he climbed on behind her. "The general has plenty of surveillance indoors and out. We'll be able to identify Warrick and track his movements from the moment he entered the house."

She wanted to believe they'd uncover proof that Warrick was a murderer, but she couldn't dismiss her nagging doubts that they'd already lost this game. She'd gone down this road with Kenneth Warrick in Afghanistan and he'd outsmarted the army investigators.

Carefully driving the motorcycle—which wasn't designed to be a dirt bike—she eased onto the packed earth trail behind the barn. Jostling along the rugged trail, the headlight bobbed in the darkness, creating small swirly comets. She was hyperaware of the man behind her. His muscular arms encircled her middle. His chest rubbed against her back. This was the closest she'd been to a man, other than her doctors and hugs from her family, since the explosion that tore her life apart. The vibration of the motorcycle engine and the slight pressure of his embrace had an impact on her that she tried to ignore. All her attention should have been concentrated on finding the killer. She'd never liked the pasty-faced Slocum but hadn't wished him dead. He had more of a grudge against her than vice versa.

At the top of a hill, she slowed the bike and then stopped. Moonlight illuminated the landscape. Glowing lights from neighboring houses glimmered across open acreage, winding roads and stands of trees. A trickling creek snaked its way through these very expensive properties.

Noah tapped her shoulder and pointed. "Over there. Do you see it?"

How could she miss the horse galloping toward them? Without dismounting from the bike, she threw off her helmet and drew her gun, waiting until the rider got close enough to take a direct shot. She didn't want to risk shooting the horse.

Gennie squinted into the night. This could be the moment when she finally confronted Warrick. Her trigger finger itched. Could she actually shoot him? Once, she had loved the man.

The figure on horseback became clear. Gennie lowered her weapon. "It's Ruby."

She and Noah both got off the bike to meet the general's wife. Gennie wasn't really into horseback riding but had to admire the black stallion with white socks and a white blaze on the face. A lot of horse, and Ruby handled him easily. Without dismounting, she looked down at them. "What's going on at the house? Why do I hear sirens?"

Noah said, "There's been a murder."

"Not Roger." Her fist covered her mouth, stifling a sob. "My God, please tell me nothing happened to my husband."

"He's fine." Noah moved closer to the dancing hooves of her horse. "The general is fine."

When Ruby peered through the night in the direction of her house, Gennie turned around. From their vantage point on the hill, she could see the Haymarket mansion with light pouring from every window and men in uniform patrolling at the perimeter. Red-and-blue police lights flashed from the front driveway.

Ruby asked, "Was it Murano?"

If she was faking this reaction, she was doing a good job of hiding her real feelings. Gennie recalled that Ruby had been an actress before she married the general. She spoke up, "It was Dean Slocum."

"Slocum? Really?" Again, her surprise seemed genuine. "What happened?"

Gennie waited for Noah to make the explanation. He was the boss and ought to be in charge. But he'd zoned out again. His reactions were slow and decidedly odd. When he was unconscious and possibly drugged, something had interrupted his usually sensible way of reasoning.

"The murder happened in the library," she said, filling the gap. "Noah was there. He was attacked and stunned. When he regained consciousness, he saw Slocum with his throat cut. The murderer was escaping on horseback, which is why we're here on the motorcycle. Have you seen anyone else riding tonight?"

"I haven't." Ruby stroked her horse's black mane. "What did the horse look like?"

"Chestnut brown," Noah said.

"And the rider?"

"I couldn't tell," he said. "There wasn't enough light."

She leaned down to stare into his face. "That means you were the last person to see Slocum alive, and, if

I'm not mistaken, you have a damned good motive for wanting the captain dead."

Ruby's words were a blow to the gut. Gennie didn't want to suspect Noah, didn't want to believe that once again she was falling for a bad man, a murderer.

Chapter Six

Standing on the trail behind the Haymarket mansion, Gennie watched the general's wife ride toward the breaking chaos at her house. She and Noah should also return to the crime scene, but she didn't want to go anywhere. Questions swarmed inside her head. Before she made a move, she wanted answers.

"Let's go." Noah donned the black helmet and patted the seat on the Yamaha.

"Where?"

"To continue the search," he said.

He had to be kidding! She shook her head and asked, "What did Ruby mean when she said you had a motive?"

"We can talk later. Right now, we've got to find the killer."

His sense of urgency was odd and unnecessary. Except for the activity at the Haymarket mansion, the surrounding landscape was serene. The waxing moon hung low in the sky. A barn owl circled overhead, a hound dog bayed and a truck bounced along a winding road through this widespread area with the monster-sized houses and five-to-ten acre lots. There was more traffic at the edge of these properties, and if Gennie had to guess, she'd figure that the man on horseback had hightailed it to the main road and used that route to disappear from sight.

"He's long gone," she said.

"You don't know that."

"He's had plenty of time to ride to a corral where he could leave his chestnut horse that you only saw from the back and couldn't really identify."

"There's more we can do. If we head in the direction of the road, we can question people along the way."

At the edge of the rugged trail, she found a knee-high boulder and sat. "An investigation needs to happen, but we aren't the ones to do it. The police will take over from here. Or the feds. Or the general might call in military cops."

"Jurisdiction is going to be a bitch," he agreed.

"In the meantime, you owe me an explanation."

He yanked the helmet off, left it on the motorcycle seat and came toward her without a single stumble. In the past few moments, his balance had improved, and his spine had straightened. It was too dark to read his expression, but she guessed that his eyes were steadier and more focused. Whatever drug he'd been given was wearing off.

Beside her small boulder, he sank to the ground and leaned his back against the stone with one leg straight out and the other bent at the knee. His upper arm touched her left thigh. She had very little sensation in the quadriceps at the front of her thigh but her hamstring was improving all the time. The slight pressure of his biceps felt so good that she adjusted her leg and subtly rubbed against him.

"You might have noticed that many of the ARC employees are former military." His voice was low and calm, as though he were talking to himself. "It's no secret that I have great respect for the discipline and training that goes into shaping the troops."

Of course, she'd noticed. One of the reasons she wanted to work at ARC was their reputation for welcoming members of the armed forces. What did this information have to do with a motive for wanting Slocum dead? "Go on."

"You might also have wondered—given my preference for military-trained agents—why I'm not a veteran."

"I never really thought about it."

When he tilted his head to look up at her, the pale moonlight highlighted his cheekbones, the straight line of his nose and his stubborn jaw. The tension in his face told her that Noah had suffered a wound—a deep emotional injury—and had not yet recovered. She had an urge to comfort him, to lean down closer to him and whisper reassurance. But she held back, aware that it would be too easy for her to slide off this rock and into his arms.

"I wanted to enlist," he said. "My older brother—ten years older than me—was an Army Ranger, and I couldn't wait to join him."

When he looked away from her, Gennie had a bad feeling about where this story was headed. "Your brother's name?"

"Josh, he was my mom's pride and joy, especially

since our oldest brother got in a lot of trouble and died from a drug overdose before his eighteenth birthday."

"I'm sorry." Unable to hold back for one more second, she placed a consoling hand on his shoulder. Though her gesture was meant to be kind and friendly, she felt a sizzle when she touched the fabric of his white shirt.

"His death nearly destroyed Mom. After 9/11 Josh enlisted in the army, and she was terrified of losing another son. She wanted him to take desk duty, but that wasn't his style. Josh stood at the front line of every charge and volunteered for every dangerous mission. I'm guessing you knew soldiers like him."

"I wasn't one of them." Though prepared to face combat, she preferred building rather than destroying. "But I stand in awe of the Rangers and the other elite teams."

"What about you? Any siblings?"

"A baby brother, he's a musician and lives with his girlfriend in Brooklyn."

"You're easy to talk to." He patted her hand, which still perched lightly on his shoulder. "When things settle down, we could spend some time together, maybe go to dinner."

"I'd like that." Her verbal response was automatic and appropriate, but her visceral reaction to the fact that Noah had asked her for a date was a flare of excitement that she quickly buried in the back of her mind. This wasn't the time for any kind of happy dance or silliness. Not only were they dealing with a murder but he was confiding in her.

"I don't like to talk about my personal stuff," he said. "It surprised me that Ruby knew so much."

Ruby's insider knowledge was no surprise. The general's wife had a talent for ferreting out bits and pieces of gossip and gathering details. She and Slocum shared that skill, and Gennie had often seen them with their heads together, giggling. "Ruby knows *everything*. She would have made an outstanding secret agent."

"I'm not hiding anything. I just like to keep things private," he said. "Twelve years ago, Josh was killed in action. Mom made me promise I wouldn't go into the armed services. That's why I didn't become a Ranger."

"I'm sorry."

"I kept that promise, even after Mom died a few years ago."

She didn't point out that a couple of years ago he would have been knocking on the door to thirty—a little old to start a career with the Rangers but still possible. "Do you still want to go into the military?"

"I'm happy where I am."

"Weren't you a cop before you joined ARC?"

"Yeah, well, Mom wasn't happy about that particular career choice, and it wasn't a great fit for me. I never made detective. When the opportunity arose at ARC, I grabbed it. Dear sweet Anna Rose was a big part of convincing my mother that I wouldn't be in danger. She was mostly correct. In my years with ARC, I've only had five serious injuries to members of my team and the people we're protecting. Slocum is the first fatality."

She'd almost forgotten how they got started on this conversation in the first place. "How does your family history connect to Slocum?"

Noah adjusted his long legs and rose to his feet. "Josh and another member of his platoon died in a covert action. They were operating under bad intelligence, given to them by Captain Dean Slocum."

Damn! Talk about a secret! "That's one hell of a motive."

He pivoted, crossed the trail and stood where he could look down at the mansion. "If I believed that Slocum had purposely caused Josh's death, I would have killed him years ago, but that's not what happened. Slocum was careless. He made a mistake."

"And you can't kill somebody for being incompetent."

"No matter how tempting."

She joined him on the path. The noise and lights from the general's mansion exploded in the still Colorado night. To the west, she saw the outline of the foothills rising into higher peaks, and thought of Noah's handsome two-story cabin. Living in the mountains made sense for a guy like him who had a surprising depth and a need for solitude. "It takes a wise man to accept and forgive a personal tragedy."

"I've accepted," he said. "But I'm no saint. I don't forgive Slocum or anybody else, from the ranking military authorities to the insurgent bastards. I won't seek revenge but I will always feel the pain of losing my brother."

"Was Slocum working for Haymarket at the time?"

"No, he was transferred shortly after his mistake. From all reports, he latched on to the general like a leech and did everything for him."

"By the time I met him," she said, "Captain Slocum was firmly attached. I've got to tell you that I'm glad the general wasn't somehow responsible for what happened to your brother."

"Maybe he was." Noah shrugged. "The military has so many levels of authority that it's nearly impossible to assign blame. You know what I mean."

"I understand."

He gazed down at her. His dark eyes gleamed like polished obsidian in the starlight. "For example, suppose you learned beyond any doubt that Warrick was responsible for the explosion that injured you and killed your team. You'd hate him. You'd curse him. But you wouldn't kill him."

"Bad example."

"Seriously, you wouldn't."

Oh, but she would. She'd fantasized about killing him slowly and painfully. If she owned irrefutable proof that Warrick was guilty, she'd be hard-pressed to hold back. Her unbridled rage clashed with the warm, pleasant feelings she was beginning to have for Noah. She shook herself and looked away from him. "We ought to get back to the house. You and I need to talk to the investigators. We're key witnesses."

"And I'm a suspect."

"Yeah, you are. You've got a motive, and you were the last person to see Slocum alive."

"Not exactly," he said. "He was dead when I saw him."

Now that his brain seemed to be functioning as usual, she wondered if his memory had improved. "Tell me about when you first went into the library."

"Again?"

"Maybe you can remember more."

"I opened the door. The room was dark." He paused.

"Not total darkness. There was light coming in through the windows. One window was open with the drape floating in the wind. I could make out forms in the shadows. Wait!" He squeezed his eyes shut, probably to concentrate. "I saw someone…just a silhouette of someone standing behind the sofa."

Anxiously, she asked, "What did this person look like?"

"Can't tell, didn't see clearly, this…person…could have been male or female."

"Tall or short? Big or small?"

He threw up his hands and shook his head. "Average, that's all I got…"

"But you're saying there were two people in the room, the one who zapped you, and the other who stood behind the sofa."

"It could have been Slocum, but I don't think so."

A second killer in the library complicated things. How had that person escaped? Were there two horses? Slocum's murder seemed to be turning into a conspiracy.

"Let's be clear on this," she said. "When you entered the room, you didn't see Slocum's body on the sofa."

"That's correct. And I didn't smell anything."

She'd been present at enough death scenes to know that the smells could be horrendous. The open window in the library might have allowed the stink of blood to dissipate. "Did you hear anything?"

"The event was in full swing with the band and lots of conversation. There were no sounds from the library. When I reached for the light switch, I got hit by a stun gun, zapped twice." He rubbed at his left side. "It's sore over here and also on my neck."

"Let me take a look." She went up on her tiptoes to see the place where he was pointing under his left ear. "Tilt your chin up."

"Don't push."

The firm skin below his short-cropped hair was marked with a bruise and twin red punctures. "Looks like you were bit by a vampire."

He winced. "It's starting to sting. Whatever drug they gave me is wearing off."

She transferred her attention to the wound on his side, lifting his untucked shirt to see the mark left behind by the stun gun. This bruise spread over a rectangular area on his rib cage; probably the attacker had hit Noah here first and hardest. She reached toward the injury but didn't touch, not wanting to cause any more pain. "First thing we do when we get back to Haymarket's house is to have the paramedics take a look at you."

"Not necessary."

"I agree that there's not a lot they can do other than give you painkillers." Which he'd probably refuse because he wanted his mind to be clear. "But it would be smart to have the EMTs draw your blood and run a tox screen."

"Why? You're not back on the thing about the poisonous flowers, are you?"

"You were drugged, Noah."

"And so?"

"You've got to start thinking like an investigator. A tox screen could indicate narcotics in your system and give a factual basis for your claim to being drugged."

"My claim?" He bristled. "You saw me staggering around. You're a witness."

"I also saw you leave a bloody handprint on the window, escaping the room where Slocum was stabbed."

"Not my finest hour."

"And I wasn't the only one," she reminded him. "Zoey was right behind me. And Mitch Murano."

"What was he doing there?"

"He chose that moment to introduce himself to me." Murano's timing was suspicious. Why was he interested in meeting her? "If he hadn't distracted me, I would have seen Kenneth Warrick enter the library."

Noah grinned. "You really don't like that guy."

"So true."

"But did he murder Slocum?"

Gennie knew she wouldn't make a good witness against Warrick because her hatred of the man was well-known. But she'd seen him. He wasn't a ghost or a figment of her imagination. He'd been in that corridor. After they reviewed the footage from the security cameras, the police would have a crystal clear picture of what happened, and Warrick would be the number one suspect.

Finally, he'd get what he deserved.

Chapter Seven

At the ambulance stationed in the driveway in front of the Haymarket mansion, a uniformed EMT seated Noah on the rear gate, lifted his shirt and prodded the bruise on his left side. "Does this hurt?"

"It's a little sore." Noah clenched his jaw. The pain was more than a twinge but not enough to make a fuss.

"I've never been hit by a stun gun." With his floppy hair and loose-lipped grin, the EMT looked much too young to be performing medical procedures. "Some of these zappers shoot a hundred-million volts. Am I right, dude?"

"Those claims are misleading. Thirty-thousand volts is just about the max." He couldn't help wincing as the kid continued to poke at him. "Electrocution is painful."

"An understatement," Gennie said. She leaned down and read the name stitched to the EMT's shirt. "You're Cody."

"Last time I checked."

"Well, Cody, I'd like your opinion. Should I take my friend to the hospital for X-rays?"

"Those ribs might be cracked," Cody said. "It might be kinda good to do X-rays."

No way. Noah refused to go to a hospital ER and wait around for the X-ray technicians to take pictures of his side. He needed to be here, facilitating the investigation. Having a murder take place while ARC handled security was a major negative for the company's reputation. This stain had to be erased as soon as possible.

"Forget my ribs," he said. "I was drugged, and I want you to draw blood and submit it for a tox screen."

"For medical reasons?" Cody asked.

"Investigative," Noah said. "I want to be able to prove I was drugged."

"Sorry, dude. No can do." Cody pushed his bangs off his forehead. "If it's part of the investigation, I need a cop to oversee the process. That's the drill. It's all about the chain of evidence and stuff."

"No problem," Gennie said. "I already talked to Tony. He's on his way to join us and he's bringing an officer with him."

Though Noah appreciated her efficiency, he wished he'd been giving the orders. Without his earbud, microphone, gun and cell phone, he felt exposed, vulnerable. And that just wasn't right. He ought to be in charge. There were about a million things he needed to do, starting with a phone call to Anna Banana.

Before he could commandeer Gennie's cell phone to make that call, he saw Tony striding along the well-lit driveway from the house. A uniformed cop accompanied him.

After a nod to Gennie, Tony asked, "What's up, boss? Are you all right?"

"I'm okay." He introduced himself to the officer and explained that Cody was going to draw blood that would be used as toxicological evidence. "I want to know what substance knocked me out."

While Cody gathered his syringe and vials, Noah asked Tony for a report.

"You go first," Tony said. "How's my bike?"

"She's fine," Gennie said as she handed over his keys. "A sweet ride."

He pocketed the keys. "Did you catch the guy on horseback?"

"Never even saw him," Gennie said.

Noah didn't want to go into details about their futile pursuit. When he talked to the investigators, he'd suggest a search of the houses in the area. "Tell me what's going on here."

"We're working with the local police," Tony said. "They're taking names from all the guests and asking questions. Nobody is allowed to leave until the primary investigators show up. I'm guessing that the FBI will be in charge."

Noah had worked with the feds before. Some were friends. Others? Not so much. "Do we know who they're sending?"

"Not yet."

"Have you spoken to the general?"

"Oh, yeah."

"And?"

"It's not good news."

Tony folded his arms across his chest and tried on a scowl. Noah remembered that Slocum referred to Tony as a *pretty boy*, and the description was apt. No matter how Tony distorted his face—crossing his dark brown eyes, sticking out his tongue or pursing his mouth like a fish—he looked like a male model. He made his un-professional outfit of jeans and a University of Colorado sweatshirt seem classy.

"Does the general have a problem?" Noah asked.

Gennie gave a short laugh. "Other than the bloody, gruesome murder of his aide?"

"Not funny." Maintaining a level of decorum was important. Slocum's death needed to be taken seriously.

"The murder upset the general," Tony said. "Not that he busted into tears or anything, but you could tell that he was sad to lose one of his men. Also, he was embarrassed in front of his fancy friends. This kind of thing isn't supposed to happen at his house."

"What else?"

"He's mad. I don't think he'll be hiring ARC again in the near future."

"He blames us," Noah said. The sad fact: the general wasn't wrong. The ARC team had failed miserably. At the very minimum, providing security meant protecting the people in the room and keeping them safe from harm. Instead, they allowed a murder to happen. Worse, the killer got away.

Sitting very still, he watched as Cody prepared to draw blood from his arm. The young EMT had an unexpectedly gentle touch with the syringe. Noah barely felt the needle slide into his vein. Crimson blood flowed through clear tubing. Cody collected three vials before he pulled out the needle and pressed a cotton ball onto the puncture site.

"Nice job," Noah said.

"Thanks, you've got good veins."

After the cop tucked the blood samples into an evidence bag, which he marked and sealed, Noah stood and took a step away from the ambulance. A rush of vertigo threatened to disorient him for a brief moment. He took a breath, concentrated and regained his equilibrium. There was no time to waste. He needed to hit the ground running. "Thanks for taking the reins, Tony. Sounds like you've done a thorough job, but I'm ready to step up and run this team. We need to rebuild ARC's reputation."

"I have a suggestion," Gennie said. "Change out of the blood-stained clothes."

He always carried a fresh shirt in his car, which was parked a short distance away from the Haymarket mansion. "Walk with me. Both of you."

The quiet in this exclusive neighborhood had been disturbed. Not that the area was seething with hectic activity. But there were vehicles driving along the winding road between the large houses and corrals. Neighbors had come onto their porches to see what was happening. The noise from the fund-raiser crowd rolled across the grounds outside the general's house like thunder before a cloudburst. Noah's pace was brisk. The farther he got from the mansion, the more his head cleared. A refreshing breeze swept through the night.

"I'll need new earbuds and a mic," he said to Tony. "Has my phone been recovered?"

"The cops found your cell phone and gun in the library. I asked if they'd give the stuff back to me, but they said no."

Noah understood. "Those items need to be processed for prints and fibers. No big deal. I've got another gun in my car, and I'll borrow a phone."

"I don't think the cops are going to return your stuff right away," Tony said as they reached the SUV. "They want to check your phone contacts and run ballistics on your gun."

"Why?" Slocum wasn't shot.

"You're a suspect, Noah."

Though he and Gennie had discussed this possibility, Noah hadn't really believed the cops would grab that conclusion. He'd been a cop and still knew guys in Denver PD, plus he'd heard that the county sheriff was a sensible guy who wouldn't rush to judgment. Still, the circumstances didn't look good. This whole thing was humiliating.

He opened the rear door of his SUV. Lucky for him, the killer hadn't taken his car keys or his wallet. In a compartment under the floor, he kept his extra weapon in a locked box. After he returned Gennie's gun, he retrieved his Glock, loaded a full clip and slipped the gun into his holster.

He straightened his shoulders. "That feels better."

"We'll clear up the suspicions as soon as we get to the house," Gennie said. "It's an easy fix. All we need to do is review the surveillance footage from the camera at the rear of the house. We'll see the real killer escaping. With a little bit of luck, we'll be able to identify him."

"Except for one thing." Tony sounded another note of doom. "The camera that was pointed toward the library window wasn't working."

"That's not possible," she said. "We verified all surveillance before the event."

"Right," Tony said. "I talked to the guy who did the

check on the outdoor cameras, and he said they were operational."

Noah didn't like the way this was shaping up. "The killer must have disabled the camera after the check was done. What about AJ on the roof? Did he see anything?"

Tony shook his head. "*Nada*, boss."

"Not even the horse? He didn't even see the horse?"

"We focused surveillance on the road and the circular driveway leading up to the house. When people started arriving, there was a lot of confusion with the valet parking guys running around and the caterers coming in and out. Even with twelve operatives, we were overwhelmed until after most of the guests arrived."

From a gym bag in the SUV, Noah took out a fresh white shirt still in the package. He didn't have another suit coat, but his gym bag held a black windbreaker to go over his shirt and hide his gun holster.

Gennie patted his arm. "You look presentable."

"Good." He appreciated her support. "I should start by talking to the person in charge."

"They're waiting for you," Tony said. "The cops need your statement. They also want to talk to Gennie. She's in almost as much trouble as you."

Her jaw dropped. "Why?"

"Nobody thinks you're the killer," Tony explained. "How could they? When you broke into the library and found the body, there were witnesses, including Murano. But they want to know why you went charging through the corridor to the library."

"I saw Kenneth Warrick," she said. "I knew he was a problem. The general told us to watch out for him.

Warrick ordered the poisonous flowers. He's the one the cops should be looking for."

"Hey, I believe you." Tony held up his hands and took a backward step. "Here's the thing. Nobody else saw this guy."

Noah had never seen anyone get so mad so fast. In an instant, her cheeks were burning with righteous fire. Her blue eyes slashed like lasers through the night.

It was his turn to support her. He linked his arm through hers. "We've got nothing to worry about. We're innocent."

"Damn right."

On the second floor of the Haymarket mansion, Gennie perched at the edge of an attractive but uncomfortable horsehair bench outside the room where interrogations were taking place. Noah had been inside for less than fifteen minutes, but time passed so slowly that it felt like she'd been sitting there for hours. Even before Noah had been taken into the room, they'd had to wait for the county sheriff who then insisted that they wait for the FBI agents who were taking over the investigation.

Though she didn't have much training or experience as a detective, she wasn't impressed with the apparent lack of procedure. Collecting information from a couple of hundred people wasn't easy, but the deputies and the police were creeping through the guest list like a pack of lethargic turtles. Almost two hours had passed since she'd picked the lock and flung open the library door. As far as she could tell, nothing much had been accomplished. They hadn't even moved Slocum's body.

The crime scene wouldn't be touched until the forensic people from the FBI arrived.

And all the while, the killer was getting farther away, laughing at them. Somebody had to take charge. It wasn't her place. But how could she stand down?

Rising from the bench, she stretched and yawned, trying to ease her tension. A high-speed sprint would have been helpful, but she settled for pacing toward the arched window at the far end of the wide hallway with white wainscoting, brass sconces and Colonial-style furniture. Looking down through the window, she saw chaos at the front entrance. It looked like some of the guests wanted to leave, and the ARC people had to dissuade them. Not a fun job.

When she pivoted and started to walk back, she saw another person at the other end of the hall. He ascended the top steps on the staircase and waved to her. Murano! She'd taken an immediate dislike to the man. Zoey's history with the self-proclaimed guru from Boulder and his version of "tough love" had disgusted Gennie. Also, Ruby thought he was a jerk. Worst of all, Murano had been careless enough to hire Kenneth Warrick.

Though she didn't know how or why Murano could be involved in the murder, her gut told her that he wasn't innocent. His hand hadn't held the knife that slashed poor Slocum's throat, but Murano could very well have been complicit, which was especially likely if Warrick, his employee, was the killer.

Tamping down her hostility, she pasted a false smile on her face and marched down the hallway to greet him. His handshake held exactly the right level of firmness.

What else would she expect from a politician? He met her gaze with guileless brown eyes.

"I'm concerned about you," he said. "Also, I'm in awe."

"Why?" she demanded.

His easy smile was charming—an annoying fact that she didn't want to acknowledge. Charisma should be an earned ability rather than a gift that seemed to be handed out indiscriminately to liars, cheats and conmen. "You've just started working for ARC," he said. "Discovering a brutally murdered man is a rough first day."

"What about the awe?"

"You charged into the library with no worries about your own personal safety, and you took immediate action. It was breathtaking."

Don't smear your false kudos on me. "Breathtaking is an overstatement. My actions were a result of my training in the army."

"In my experience with former military personnel, I've found that they're often hesitant, unwilling to act unless someone else gives the orders. That's not you, Gennie. You're strong, a natural leader."

Too many compliments. What did he want from her? "Why did you come up here, Dr. Murano? Were you looking for me?"

"Call me Mitch." He flashed another smile. His whitened teeth stood out against his swarthy complexion. "Though I'm delighted to run into you, I came up here hoping to talk to the FBI. It's getting late, and I hoped that we could have permission to leave."

It seemed like a reasonable excuse. Was she overreacting? "The investigators are talking to Noah right now. They should be done soon."

"May I wait with you?" he asked as he touched the decorative clasp for his bolo tie. "Earlier when we spoke, I mentioned my interest in your insensitivity to pain."

"Have a seat." She gestured to the uncomfortable bench. "My physical condition really isn't all that interesting."

With perfect posture, he sat and straightened the crease on his trousers. Though she didn't like him or trust him, she had to admit that Mitch Murano was neat and well groomed. A few strands of gray swirled through his shoulder-length black hair and his features were symmetrical. It'd be difficult to pin down his age. If she had to guess, she'd say he was somewhere between forty-five and sixty.

"The general told me about your injuries," he said. "You don't feel pain in parts of your arms and legs as a result of nerve damage and neurological complications from concussions."

"Yes." She didn't provide him with more details.

"Using a combination of medical procedures and physical therapy, you've regained much of the function in your limbs."

"Yes." Again, she was terse. Knowledge was power, and she didn't want to give Murano the edge.

"Perhaps I could suggest a more metaphysical approach to your condition," he said.

She wasn't opposed to alternative medicine, far from it. She meditated regularly, had a monthly session with an acupuncturist, preferred herbal remedies and knew enough about plants to gather her own herbs from the mountains. "I try to keep an open mind."

"As do I," he said. "At MIME—that's the acronym for Murano Institute for Meditation and Enlightenment—I've had great success working with people who suffer from a variety of ailments that range from headaches to cancer tumors. I'd like to study you, to help you."

There was the hook! If she'd been a cooperative little minnow, she would have swallowed it whole, but she was wary. "I'll think about it."

Murano had perfected the art of seeming sincere. He held his hand toward her. "Please, Gennie, let me heal your wounds."

Ignoring his outstretched hand would have been rude, but accepting a handshake implied consent. She tried to maintain control by clasping his hand between both of hers. "A generous offer," she said and quickly withdrew, rising to her feet and taking a step away from him. "I have a few questions for you. Do you mind?"

"Ask whatever you wish."

She'd start with Warrick. Murano's unsolicited offer of help opened the door, and she intended to storm through before he had a chance to change his mind. Taking her cell phone from the pocket of her jumpsuit, she scrolled to the photo of Warrick that Noah had sent earlier in the evening. She held it so Murano could see. "Do you recognize this man?"

"He looks familiar."

When she'd seen Warrick, he'd made adjustments to his appearance. "Imagine him with a neatly trimmed beard, streaked blond hair and dark eyebrows."

Murano squinted and shook his head. "What's his name?"

Instead of using the alias, she went for it. "Kenneth Warrick. He works for you."

"I don't keep track of each and every one of my employees. It might help if you tell me what this man means to you."

Aware that he was playing her, she struggled to keep her face expressionless. She should have prepared a cover story, but she'd never been good at lying. "Three years ago, I knew him in Afghanistan."

"I understand." Murano stroked his chin and nodded. "General Haymarket mentioned that you had an unfortunate relationship during your tour of duty. You suspected your lover of betraying you and your platoon. Is that your connection to Kenneth Warrick?"

She refused to be manipulated. "Do you recognize him?"

"You want revenge, don't you?" He stood and glided toward her. He came too close, as though daring her to retreat. "Vengeance is poisoning your thinking and slowing your recovery. I can show you how to let it go."

"Back off." She pushed her fingertips into his chest. "I saw Kenneth Warrick today. He was headed toward the library."

The door to the interrogation room swung open, and Noah stepped into the hallway followed by one of the FBI agents. She could tell that the interview hadn't gone well. Anger radiated from Noah, and his jaw was clenched.

Still, she couldn't help asking, "Are we in the clear? Has the data from the surveillance cameras been reviewed? I know the one from the rear of the house was disabled, but what about the indoor cameras?"

He shook his head. "There was no sign of Warrick."

"That can't be. I saw him."

Murano leaned toward her and said, "The mind operates in curious ways. Perhaps you wanted to see him."

"Wrong. He's the last person on earth that I want to be with."

"Is he?"

When the supposed guru touched her shoulder, she slapped his hand away. "With all due respect, I already told you to back off."

He held one of his engraved business cards toward her. "You need my help, Gennie."

She'd rather kiss a tarantula than accept *anything* from Murano. Ignoring the card he pushed toward her, she turned her back and marched into the FBI interrogation room.

Chapter Eight

Gennie's interview with the FBI piled one layer of frustration upon another until they'd constructed a solid wall between them with no chance of actual communication. She wanted to help, really she did. But they thwarted her at every turn, saying over and over that there was no way for Kenneth Warrick to be in the house and not show up on any of the surveillance cameras. Therefore, she must be mistaken.

But she wasn't.

Since the agents refused to believe she saw Warrick, they couldn't understand her actions. Why did she put out an alert to the ARC team without sending a photo? What was her thing with poisonous flowers? Why had she rushed to the library and picked the lock? Their conclusion was insulting: she must be delusional. One of the agents referenced her prior relationship with Warrick and suggested that she was a lovesick, jilted woman pining for her former fiancé.

Oh hell, no.

And why had she commandeered Tony's motorcycle and taken off with Noah? That explanation was less embarrassing for her when she told them that Noah was giving the orders. Unfortunately, her answers made him look unreliable because she hadn't seen the killer making his escape. Nor had she seen the horse he rode in on.

Her interview ended with a curt dismissal and a warning. The feds told her that she was free to go but shouldn't leave town because they'd have more questions for her.

She stepped into the hallway, dreading the possibility of running into Murano again. Instead, Noah was waiting. Overwhelmed by relief, she felt like throwing herself into his arms but was mindful of the feds who stood in the doorway watching. Side by side, she and Noah marched toward the staircase.

"We're out of here," he said.

"I'm so ready."

As they exited the mansion, he told her that he'd left Tony in charge of a skeleton crew. Most of the ARC personnel had been dismissed after their interviews. With all the other law enforcement personnel keeping watch, the services of a private security firm were redundant, especially since the guests were also being sent home.

She inhaled a breath of fresh night air, glad to be leaving the hive of activity at the mansion but still frustrated. "The FBI guys didn't believe a word I said."

"Same here."

"That leaves me with an obvious conclusion," she said.

"Tell me."

"We need to solve this crime ourselves." She'd be damned if she allowed Warrick to get away with murder again. In Afghanistan, she'd been incapacitated and unable to investigate. This time, she happened to be in the right place at the right time with the right resources. So what if the feds didn't believe her? She would make it her business to prove his guilt. "Do you agree, Noah?"

"I'm motivated. Being a suspect doesn't sit well with me."

"Where do we start?"

"We find out what was on the security cams," he said. "That means calling in the big gun, the genius, the best cyber-analyst west of the Mississippi. She's waiting for us at the ARC office."

Gennie whispered, "Yay," and did a subtle fist pump. Anna Rose Claymore, the founder of ARC was a legend. Trained by the CIA and by NORAD in Colorado Springs, she'd been active in cybersecurity for over twenty years while raising five children and overseeing ARC's business. If anybody could figure out what was on those cameras, she could. "Has there ever before been a murder at an event where ARC was providing security?"

"Not to my knowledge," he said. "I was hired eleven years ago when Anna's husband, David, was running the field operations. Since then, we've had a couple serious injuries, but no one died."

"Will Anna Rose be upset?"

"You bet. ARC is David's legacy. As such, the company is nearly as important to her as her kids or her grandchildren. She'll want this murder solved and ARC's impeccable reputation restored."

For the first time since she saw Warrick in the ballroom, Gennie dared to hope that things would turn out right. She, Noah and Anna Rose were on the same page, and they were a force to be reckoned with.

Since she'd carpooled with Zoey to the mansion, she rode with Noah to the ARC office where she'd left her car. The building—a square six-story structure south of Denver—wasn't particularly attractive or interesting, but ARC's underground parking included a full floor with high-level security protection. A fleet of motor-cycles, Hummers, SUVs and bulletproof vehicles were lined up and ready to roll.

Noah parked his SUV beside a reinforced bullet-proof limo with tinted windows and a high performance V10 engine. She stroked the gleaming ebony fender. "A handsome vehicle, I've heard it's not only fast but al-most indestructible. When do I get to drive this baby?"

"We save Black Beauty for international bigwigs, and you'll have to fight Tony for the car keys."

They took the elevator to the second floor. To the left was a gym. To the right were the actual offices with open space, desks and conference rooms. Behind a purple door was the cyber area containing communica-tion devices, computers, monitors and other electronic equipment. In a spacious corner office, Anna Rose sat in the middle of a U-shaped desk area surrounded by computer equipment and a lifetime accumulation of goofy little Mother's Day gifts from her brood.

When they entered, she bounded from her chair and gathered them both in her arms for a quick but generous hug. She was pleasantly soft and smelled like vanilla cookies. Beaming at Gennie, she pushed her polka-dot glasses up on her nose and said, "Welcome to my lair."

Though they'd met on Gennie's first full day at ARC, they'd never had time to chat, and Gennie had never been invited into the inner sanctum. Her first impression of the room made her think of a wild, crazy circus, but she noticed a logical order in the arrangement of personal and professional objects. The desk area was devoted to computers and screens. There was a small kitchenette. Floor-to-ceiling shelves behind a sofa and coffee table were filled with handmade baskets in a multitude of colors, dozens of plastic roses and an army of ceramic critters.

Anna Rose pointed to the neon green sofa with orange and gold pillows. "Sit."

Gennie was happy to oblige. Noah sat beside her with his long legs out in front of him. He unfolded his arms over his head and yawned, obviously comfortable in the company of Anna Rose.

"First, you eat," she said as she filled the coffee table with a plate of turkey sandwiches, a fruit salad and bottled water from a mini-fridge. "I'm sure you didn't have a chance to nibble at the big event."

Until this moment, Gennie hadn't realized how hungry she was. When Anna Rose added a plate of cookies to the spread on the coffee table, she almost swooned. "Thank you."

"My poor lamb! You've had a rough first day at work but don't worry. Things will get better."

Gennie believed this eclectic grandma with the blue-streaked hair. Anna Rose was magic. She could wave a wand and make everything good. Gennie took a bite of the cookie. It was warm! She glanced over at Noah who had already scarfed down his sandwich.

"Were you able to access the data on the security cams?" he asked.

"That was my first move." Anna Rose sat primly

on a zebra-striped chair and aimed a remote control at a giant monitor hanging on the wall opposite the sofa. Twenty-four transmissions from security cameras at the Haymarket mansion splashed across the screen in a dizzying kaleidoscope of images.

Gennie squinted. "I'm surprised the FBI let you have this."

"They don't exactly know what I have, dear. Eight minutes ago, they closed down the cams. A rude move if you ask me…and futile. I can still hack in if I want."

"We're not breaking any rules," Noah assured her. "When we took this job for the general, his security people gave us the codes that allowed Anna Rose to read these cameras."

She pressed buttons on the remote and zoomed in on a single image that she enlarged until it took up much of the screen. "This one is important."

The rear view of the mansion focused on the library windows and had been recorded from a second-floor camera. "Can we see inside?" Gennie asked. "The lights are on."

"Oh, I've tried." Anna Rose paced at the edge of the monitor. "There's a curtain, and reflection from the outdoor lights that automatically come on when it starts to get dark."

"What time was this taken?"

"Read the time stamp in the corner. It's 7:07, the edge of sunset."

Noah said, "Long before I entered the library."

As they watched, the image on the screen went dead.

Anna Rose flipped through several functions, trying to bring the picture back while she explained. "This malfunction wasn't caused by a technological glitch. The blackout was due to brute force. The camera took a bullet to the lens."

"I don't suppose any of the other cameras show the shooter," Noah said.

"Unfortunately, no." Anna Rose scowled at the screen. "Nor does any of the surveillance show the horse. Sorry, Noah."

"I figured that would happen." He picked up another cookie. "The reins were probably tethered to a shrub that was out of camera range."

After Anna Rose punched a few buttons, the large monitor returned to the original display from twenty-four surveillance cameras. While eating her sandwich, Gennie concentrated on one image at a time, trying to catch a glimpse of Warrick among the other partygoers. She recalled the details of his new appearance. His hair was long, dyed blond and tied in a ponytail at his nape. Thick blond scruff disguised his weak chin. His outfit would blend into almost any Colorado gathering: sports jacket, polo shirt and jeans. Had he been armed? She'd only seen him for a second and hadn't noticed a holster.

If he'd shot the camera, he had to be armed. They should have used metal detectors at the entrance. Slocum was to blame for allowing the guests to carry weapons. Even if the feds confiscated all the guns and ran ballistics, they wouldn't have Warrick's piece, damn him.

Munching on a second cookie, she listened while Anna Rose and Noah constructed a timeline for the murder. When Noah received the phone call, Slocum must have already been in the library. The lights in the room were on and, most likely, the murderer was with him.

Gennie piped up, "That means he knew the killer."

They all three nodded. Slocum had been fastidious, snarky and smug—not the sort of person who inspired sympathy. But she couldn't help feeling sorry for him. He'd been killed by someone he trusted. When had Slocum guessed what was about to happen? Had he seen death coming?

"I think he was killed before the lights went out," Noah said. "There might have been an accomplice in the room."

Anna Rose widened her eyes behind her colorful frames. "Two people in the room? That's very interesting, dear. And it would explain how so much was accomplished in the few minutes between when Noah got the call and when he opened the door. They incapacitated Slocum, opened the window, shot the camera, turned out the light and prepared to ambush Noah with a stun gun. Yes, indeed, I like the two-man concept."

Noah nodded toward Gennie. "You've been looking at the images. Have you seen Warrick?"

"I'm afraid not. I wish I'd had the presence of mind to snap a picture of him, but he was moving fast, dodging between the French doors at the library corridor."

"An area without a camera." Anna Rose shook her head and made a tsk sound. "We really should talk to the general about updating his security systems. That is, if he ever speaks to us again."

"Let's get back to the timeline." Noah stood, stretched and winced. The aftereffects of a stun gun assault had to be painful. When he paced between the sofa and the monitor, she noticed a hitch in his stride. "Gennie, what time did you see Warrick?"

"Easy enough to check." She took out her cell phone and viewed the history. "I sent an alert to the rest of the team at 7:34, which was after the camera went dead and before you entered the library. Is it possible that you went into the library before Warrick?"

"There are too many alternatives." Anna Rose exhaled a sigh and sank into her zebra chair. "We can't break this down minute by minute, not without the facts. All we know for sure is that Noah and one or two other people were in the room with Slocum when he died. Someone locked the door. The camera went dead. And Gennie picked the lock."

"Here's another fact," Noah said. "I didn't do it."

"Of course not, dear. That goes without saying."

The hopeful atmosphere in the office was deflating like a slow leak in a tire, and Gennie was reminded of how she'd felt during the investigation of Warrick in Afghanistan. That couldn't, wouldn't happen again. "My instincts tell me that Kenneth Warrick is the killer. We have to find evidence. We can't let him get away."

Anna Rose spoke in the tone of a grandma making crafts. "Let's start with the obvious question, shall we? How did Mr. Warrick get into the house without appearing on a camera?"

"He might have been inside earlier," Noah said. "Maybe he was hiding?"

"Or using a complicated disguise," Gennie said. "He might have known how to avoid the cameras."

"You knew him well," Anna Rose said. "What sort of man is he?"

Pushing aside her anger, she tried to come up with an accurate portrait. "He's smart but not as clever as he thinks he is. And he's confident, thinks of himself as an alpha. Most of all, he hates criticism and always needs to be right, even if he has to cheat and lie to win."

"And when he loses?"

"He's a vengeful bastard."

Anna Rose asked, "How does he feel about you?"

She leaned back against the sofa, closed her eyes and cast her mind into another lifetime when she'd been stationed in Afghanistan working in the Army Corps of Engineers. After the bomb, she'd hated Warrick. According to people who were close to the investigation, he blamed her for losing his position as a private contractor. "He doesn't much like me."

"Revenge is a terrible thing." Anna Rose looked toward Noah. "As we proceed, we need to be mindful of the potential danger, both to Gennie and to you."

"Me?" He sounded surprised.

"This killer has gone to a great deal of trouble to frame you, dear. And, I must say, he or she has done a rather good job of implicating you in this murder." Bouncing to her feet, she swept toward the door to her office and opened it wide. "Go home, get some sleep and we'll start fresh in the morning."

"Wait," Gennie said. "I know how he got to the library without being picked up by a camera."

WHEN SHE AND Noah entered the underground parking area, Gennie was still patting herself on the back. She'd figured out a piece of this complicated murder, starting with the premise that Warrick was part of the twosome that killed Slocum. This led to the logical question: why plan an escape on horseback?

The answer: because the killer arrived on horseback in order to avoid being seen by cameras or security personnel. In the early part of the evening, ARC had concentrated on the front entrance. The killer had taken advantage by riding to the rear of the house, leaving his horse out of range, shooting out the camera and entering through the window. He escaped the same way.

Noah walked her to her car. "If Warrick got into and out of the house the way you think he did, why did he leave the library? Why parade around in the ballroom where you could see him."

"Didn't I already tell you that he's a vengeful bastard?" He'd shown himself to her, only to her. "His disappearing act and the poisonous flowers made me look like a lunatic. The FBI won't believe anything I say."

"He could have been meeting someone else," Noah said.

"It's possible." She clicked open the lock on her Land Rover. "That would mean three people were involved in the murder. It's practically a conspiracy."

"Slocum made a lot of people angry." He held her door as she climbed inside. "I'm thinking about what Anna Rose said. There's danger attached to this murder. What kind of security do you have at your house?"

Her parents' house was in a quiet neighborhood in north Denver. They'd never felt a need for surveillance cameras. "I lock the doors when I leave."

"Windows?"

"I think I left a couple open. The weather has been nice and—"

"Would you like to spend the night at my condo?"

She eyed him curiously. The sandwiches and cookies had revived them both, but Noah still looked tired. If anybody needed backup protection, it was him. "I'll be okay."

"If you change your mind, call me." He closed her car door and stepped back, watching as she pulled out of the slot and drove to the exit.

His offer of help was hugely unnecessary and a little bit insulting. Would Noah have made the same offer if she were a man? She had the training and the qualifications to take care of herself in almost any circumstance.

But her parents' brick house—two stories, three bedrooms, a huge study and a giant spruce tree in the front yard—wasn't a fortress. She should be alert to possible danger. Though she wasn't looking for a fight, she hoped Warrick would try something as stupid as breaking into her home. She welcomed a confrontation with him. He could choose the weapon, and she would win the battle.

Her Land Rover merged easily onto the I-25 highway. At this time of night, there wasn't much traffic, and she was making good time. Not as tired as she thought she'd be but grungy. She was looking forward to a long hot shower. Tomorrow would be a difficult day, not so much for her but for Noah. The FBI guys hadn't been subtle about naming him as a suspect, especially since he had a motive.

There had to be others who had hated Slocum. He wasn't a charming person. But hate was different from murder. Why had Warrick wanted the captain dead?

Was the attack personal? Maybe Warrick was a contract killer, paid to kill Slocum by Murano.

Contemplating the many possibilities, she pulled into the driveway to the left of her parents' house and parked. Because she hadn't yet picked up the mail today, she went around to the wide front porch where her mom and dad often sat in their rocking chairs. They claimed to be happy in Phoenix but she heard a longing in their voices when they talked about Denver.

When she reached into the mailbox, she heard a creaking sound. It came from inside the house. Gennie dropped the mail and drew her Beretta.

Chapter Nine

Parked at the curb halfway up the street from Gennie's house, Noah peered through his windshield. Following her home might have been an overreaction on his part, but he hadn't wanted to take any chances. Anna Rose had given them a clear warning, and she was usually right. Slocum's murder could lead to danger for Gennie.

Noah would make sure she got safely inside her house, and then he'd leave. No harm done.

With the streetlights and the glow from some of her neighbors' houses, his field of vision would have been excellent if it hadn't been for the towering spruce tree in her front yard. He'd seen her park in the driveway and walk toward her porch and then she disappeared in the shadow of the tree that was as tall as the roof of her two-story house. Had she gone inside? If so, why hadn't she turned on the lights? That damn tree made it impossible to see what was going on. He turned off the interior light in his SUV, slipped through the door and carefully approached her house.

When he was close enough to see the porch, he noticed that the front door was open.

He heard two gunshots, rapid fire.

Dashing across her lawn, he passed a row of daffodils at the edge of her porch.

From inside the house, a female voice cried out. "Don't shoot! I'm unarmed."

Gennie responded. "You've got three seconds to show yourself. One...two..."

"It's me, Ruby."

Noah halted on the porch. Through the open door, he saw Gennie crouched behind an overstuffed chair. She reacted to his presence with an angry growl, and then she snapped an order. "Cover her."

He stepped through the front door. With his Glock braced in both hands, he focused on Ruby Haymarket who stood in the middle of the room with her hands raised above her head. What the hell was she doing here?

Gennie turned on a floor lamp beside a bulky tweed sofa. All the furniture in her parents' house seemed thick and solid as though rooted in this room with hardwood floors and oak bookshelves. Nearly every flat surface held a big healthy potted plant. Gennie flicked a switch to turn on the overhead light in the adjoining dining room, came back to Ruby and started frisking her.

"Hey!" The general's wife slapped at Gennie's hands. "What do you think you're doing?"

"Searching you for weapons. You broke into my house."

"It's not like I breached some kind of sophisticated security. A window in the back bedroom was open. I pulled over a lawn chair, popped off the screen and climbed through."

"Why?" Gennie demanded.

"I need your help."

Clearly annoyed, Gennie glared at him. "What are you doing here?"

Since he didn't have a good excuse, he tried the truth. "I was worried about you."

"Without cause, as you can plainly see." She gestured to the wide-bodied chairs. "Let's all sit down. Ruby, you can tell us why you need our help."

"Not both of you."

"Whatever you say to me, you can say to Noah."

"Fine." When Ruby sank into the chair, the bulky arms nearly smothered her. "I need you, Gennie. I want you to come home with me and be my bodyguard."

"That's not how things work at ARC," Noah said. "You make a request, and I make the assignment."

"This isn't an ARC project," she said archly. "It's not likely that my husband will ever hire your company again, Noah. He's so mad at you that he almost believes the FBI theory that you killed Slocum. Everybody knows that you two hated each other."

Noah held his anger in check. No point in arguing with Ruby—he didn't owe her an explanation. "Gennie works for me."

"I want to hire her for a private assignment."

"Why?" Gennie sank onto the sofa. The soft glimmer from the lamp burnished her blond curls and highlighted her cheekbones. Looking at her made him feel better. Though her day had been long and complicated, she didn't show the signs of exhaustion. Her eyes were bright and alert. She was alive, vivacious.

"I'm afraid," Ruby said in a small voice. She sounded like a child, which either meant she was really alarmed or she was a clever actress, playing on Gennie's kind nature to get her way. Knowing Ruby, he leaned toward the latter.

"I've known you for a long time," Gennie said. "You're not the type who scares easily."

"Please, will you help me?"

"I need more information."

"It's the next of kin," she said. "Slocum's brother, Buddy, and his wife are coming here to take care of things, and I'm afraid they're going to cause trouble. There's no need for them to be here. Slocum wanted a military funeral, and Roger will arrange for the honor guard and the twenty-one-gun salute."

In his work with other wealthy clients who were often as self-absorbed as Ruby, Noah had developed a numbing sense of patience. Though it seemed impossible that the general's wife would be frightened by the family of a recently murdered man, he didn't comment. Instead, he nodded and murmured, "Uh-huh."

"They're his only living survivors," she said. "They're from Nashville."

Not scary. "Uh-huh."

"I talked to the wife on the phone," Ruby said. "She threatened me."

Still not scary but interesting. Noah sat up straighter. "Uh-huh."

"This woman, Dean Slocum's sister-in-law, said that Dean had told her everything."

"Everything?" Noah felt himself being drawn in to Ruby's story. He was almost hooked. "What did she know?"

"She said if I didn't play along..."

Ruby's voice faded. She covered her face with her hands, and her shoulders trembled. *Too much!* She'd overplayed her hand with the weeping and moaning. He'd seen fake tears too many times before.

Obviously, Gennie didn't share his cynicism. She left the sofa and went to Ruby. Stroking her back, she whispered assurances. He really hoped she wouldn't be drawn into this scheme by Ruby's Oscar-winning performance.

The best way to get at the truth would be for him to talk to Ruby alone. "Gennie, maybe we could all use a cup of tea."

"Good idea. I have an herbal blend with chamomile that's really soothing." She gave Ruby a final pat and spoke gently to her. "Don't worry. I'll be back in a sec."

He noticed Ruby frowning at Gennie's back as she crossed the dining room and entered the kitchen. Though fairly certain that the tears were an act, he wanted to find out if she had a real cause for fear. Under the guise of handing her a tissue, he went to the chair where she was sitting. While she dabbed at her eyes, he pulled an ottoman close and sat facing her. Their knees were almost touching.

"I don't know what you're really after, Ruby, but it's not fair to play on Gennie's sympathy. I won't let you use her."

"That's not your call."

"Oh, but it is," he said. "Gennie was trained in the army."

"Don't you think I know that?"

"One of the first and strongest lessons learned by

a new recruit is loyalty. Ask your husband. Loyalty counts for a lot."

"So what?"

"Gennie works for me now. In a way, I'm her commanding officer." Never would he say that to her face. "She's obliged to follow my orders. If I tell her not to work for you, she won't."

"You think you're clever, but her first loyalty goes to my husband."

Not the way he'd heard the story. The general had brought Gennie's military career to a screeching halt, and she wasn't inclined to forgive him. "Are you sure about that?"

"Even if she doesn't like Roger, he trusts her and respects her opinion." Her eyes narrowed to dark slits as she glared. "You're right about one thing. I plan to use Gennie but not for any cruel or devious reason. I need her support. If she's on my team, Roger will pay attention."

And that sounded more like the truth. "What does the sister-in-law have on you?"

"It's ridiculous." She massaged her temples and raked her fingers through her dark blond hair. "Loretta—that's her name—claims to have proof that I was intimate with Dean Slocum."

Noah hadn't seen that one coming. His impression was that Ruby and Slocum barely tolerated each other. "An affair?"

"She called me a gold digger and said I was after her brother-in-law's money. Unbelievable! I live in a mansion, drive a Jag, have three horses and jewelry appraised in the millions of dollars. Roger has provided me with a fantastic lifestyle." This time, the tear that trickled down her cheek was real. "And I love him."

In spite of her crazy behavior and her fake weeping, Noah believed that she was honestly worried about the threat to her marriage. Not because of the money. Ruby was scared of losing her life partner.

Carrying a tray with a steeping pot of tea, a container of honey and another of milk, Gennie emerged from the kitchen. In the dining room, she placed the tray on the table, stepped back and said, "I'll help you, Ruby. But you need to be honest with me."

"I will."

"Come in here and have some chamomile." She motioned for both of them to join her. "Noah and I need to figure out who killed Slocum, and I think you can help us."

Ruby nodded vigorously as she took the seat at the head of the carved oak table with green placemats and daffodils in a small vase. "Ask me anything."

"I overheard what you and Noah were talking about," Gennie admitted. "I'm surprised that Loretta thought Dean Slocum was so rich. Did she happen to mention his net worth?"

"You bet she did. She said it was over $1.23 million plus three properties in Denver." Ruby accepted a cup of tea and stirred in a dollop of milk. "I had the feeling that she and the brother kept close watch on Slocum's finances. As next of kin, they're the heirs."

"Unless he made a will," Noah pointed out, "and named someone else as his beneficiary. Is that why Loretta is mad at you? She thought you'd get a piece of the inheritance."

Gennie prepared her own cup of tea. "I never would have guessed that Slocum was a millionaire. How did he get all that money?"

"Well, it wasn't family wealth." Ruby sipped her tea. "I met Buddy a couple of times before, and he is most definitely not a rich man. Actually, I liked him. Buddy is a friendly guy whose easygoing personality is the opposite of Dean's uptight, perfectionist attitude. Loretta is a lot more like Dean than his brother."

Noah sat back and listened while Ruby spilled the little she knew about the Slocum family. His brain had stuck on the $1.23 million. That kind of money provided a big juicy motive for murder, especially for the next of kin.

There was a good chance that Slocum had amassed his fortune through illegal means. The buying and selling of illegal arms came immediately to mind. Gennie's nemesis, Warrick, had been a private contractor and would have the connections necessary to move illegal arms. Slocum's murder could have been a falling out among thieves.

Gennie cleared her throat. "I didn't quite hear this from the kitchen, but you mentioned an affair."

"Ridiculous," Ruby muttered.

"What kind of proof does Loretta have?"

Ruby held a napkin in front of her mouth. Her eyes darted. "There was a letter."

Gennie sat back and waited, stirring her tea and taking ladylike sips.

Ruby blurted. "The letter never mentioned any names. And it wasn't about an affair, just a kiss. I was foolish. I kissed him before I knew what I was doing.

Then I came to my senses and wrote the letter saying we should never see each other again."

"And Loretta has the letter," Gennie said. "How did she get her paws on it?"

"I don't know."

"It's hard to believe you kissed Dean Slocum."

"Because I didn't."

"Who was the man?" Gennie asked.

Ruby stared into her teacup. "Kenneth Warrick."

The silence that followed her announcement blanketed the dining room with a suffocating, ominous darkness. He could have sworn that for an instant the lights blinked out and showed him a glimpse of hell where Warrick wielded a pitchfork. Noah was impressed by Gennie's ability to stay calm. She'd been hurt by Warrick but didn't allow her pain to show.

In measured tones, she asked, "How did you meet him?"

"I'm so sorry, Gennie. I know you were involved with Warrick."

"Not anymore." Gennie raised her teacup to her lips and took a sip. "Did you meet Warrick when you were taking a class with Murano?"

"At the Institute in Boulder," she said, bobbing her head. "Warrick was using a different name but I remembered meeting him in Afghanistan. Forgive me for saying this, Gennie, but he's still a good-looking man. When I recognized him, he begged me not to tell my husband because he didn't want to lose his job with Murano."

"You believed him," Noah said. "You didn't suspect him of working a scam."

"I was conned," she admitted. "I wouldn't expect you to understand, Noah, but there's something very appealing about a *bad boy*. When Warrick asked me to give him a chance, I couldn't resist. Before I knew what was happening, we were kissing."

"What's done is done," Gennie said. "I'll come to the mansion tomorrow in the morning before Loretta and Buddy arrive. And I need to bring Noah."

"I suppose that's all right," Ruby said. "I need to talk to my husband."

Noah had another question. "Did Slocum ever ask you for money?"

"What do you mean?"

"Blackmail."

"Never," she said.

"Why would he hold back on such a valuable, dangerous secret?"

"Slocum knew that if he showed the letter to Roger and the general had to choose between him and me, I'd come out on top."

Still, he'd held on to that incriminating letter. And he'd sent it to his in-laws for safekeeping. *Why?* Noah had a feeling that the explanation wasn't going to be pretty.

Chapter Ten

At Noah's condo, Gennie stepped through the sliding glass door onto the sixteenth-floor balcony. The bright lights of downtown Denver clustered in a knot and then spread toward the shadow of distant peaks to the west. Though she'd never been a huge fan of urban living, the view was mesmerizing—twinkling house lights, neon signs on stores, headlights and taillights that came and went into the night.

The interior of the condo was also impressive, in spite of the total lack of houseplants. Noah's furniture was modern, and his artwork showed eclectic influences, ranging from realistic nature paintings to modernist color blocks and streaky abstracts of athletes. When she complimented him, he was honest enough to tell her that his ex-wife had chosen most of the art. Typically, Gennie avoided divorced men because they tended to be bitter. Noah was different. He and his wife had only been married two years and both acknowledged that it was a mistake. They stayed friends but she moved back east.

Ever since she met Noah, she'd been thinking about what would happen if they actually went on a date. Having a romantic relationship with the boss seemed like a terrible idea, but here she was in his condo, preparing to spend the night. *Keep it professional, Gennie.* She had loads of experience being in close contact with male coworkers and not getting involved with them; she had perfected the ability to be "just one of the guys."

That was what she needed with Noah. They could be friends, colleagues, people who worked together and not lovers, which didn't mean she shouldn't appreciate the good things about him. This condo was pretty great.

Resting her forearms on the balcony railing, she watched three helicopters swoop across the sky like oversized nocturnal dragonflies. She felt wide-awake and alert, churning with energy when she really should have been exhausted. The day's physical activity had been a challenge, and her stress level was off the charts. Part of that tension could be attributed to her inappropriate attraction to Noah, but mostly she was upset by the murder.

No matter how she looked at the death of Slocum, she saw connections to Kenneth Warrick. Would he never cease to cause turmoil in her life? After returning to the states, she never expected to see him again. But here he was! Once again, he hovered over her life like a monster spider—big, bold and nasty.

Noah joined her on the balcony and handed her a glass of merlot. He raised his for a toast. "Welcome to your first day at ARC Security."

Holding up her wine, she gazed at him over the rim of the glass. Moonlight softened the chiseled line of his jaw and gleamed in his eyes. Drinking wine made this moment feel more intimate than it should have been, but it was too late for coffee, and she'd had her fill of tea. What the hell, the wine would help her sleep. "Cheers!"

"I'm glad you decided to spend the night here."

"So am I." The merlot slid easily down her throat. "Obviously, my house isn't secure. If Ruby Haymarket can break in, anybody can. I'm a little embarrassed that I haven't taken precautions. I used to pester my parents about setting up a security system, and now I'm as careless as they were."

"Lucky for you," he said, "security is our business. Tomorrow, we'll get a technician to upgrade your locks, install alarm sensors and set up surveillance equipment."

Adding security wasn't the only change she wanted to make at her parents' house. The super-heavy furniture and clunky wood accessories weren't her taste. The wallpaper had to go, and the kitchen needed renovating. Gennie was ready to roll, but these projects required the approval of her parents and her musician brother who had a say in what happened to the family legacy even though he lived in New York. Consulting with them brought Gennie's initiative to a dead stop. Instead of a total remodel, she'd settle for recreating the landscaping by planting veggies and more flowers. And she definitely wanted to get rid of the giant spruce tree in the front—a major project.

"How long are you watching the house for your parents?" he asked.

"Maybe forever. I doubt that they're coming back to Denver. Mama and Papa Fox have officially joined the ranks of the snowbirds in sunny Phoenix."

"It's a nice property," he said. "Do you ever think of selling?"

"To tell the truth, I'd like for them to sell the family homestead. I've got enough saved for a down payment for my own place."

"House or condo?"

"House," she said emphatically. "Don't get me wrong, I love your view. And the extra protection in a condo building comes in handy, especially if I travel. But I need a yard."

"To plant your flowers," he said.

"Like Mary, Mary, quite contrary. My brother teases me with that rhyme. Every time we meet, he asks, how does your garden grow?"

"With daffodils," Noah said. "You had some in the front yard and more in a vase."

"In the language of flowers, daffodils are supposed to be welcoming and lucky. They're a perfect flower for an entrance—a fresh springtime bloom."

"So what happens to your good fortune in the late summer and fall?"

"Any plant that makes me smile is good luck. Daisies and pansies are cheerful. Roses are beautiful and sometimes they smell good. And I do enjoy a honeysuckle vine." She couldn't believe she was having this girly conversation with her very masculine boss. "Are you into gardening?"

"Not for me, but I like your passion for flowers. You must have hated Afghanistan. That's not a part of the world known for pretty posies."

"The natural beauty is there. You just have to know where to look for it."

"That's a solid philosophy." He tasted his wine and cocked his head to one side. "Reminds me of that song, 'Always Look on the Bright Side of Life' from that Monty Python movie. Do you remember it?"

"Are you being ironic?"

"Maybe."

Gennie couldn't take credit for her sunny outlook. Optimism came naturally to her, which was probably the result of growing up in a loving family with few disappointments and even fewer tragedies. When she was older, she'd followed her dream of becoming an engineer and had done well at Texas A&M. "I've had a fortunate life."

"Is that so?" His voice sounded a cynical note. "If you're so lucky, how do you explain being betrayed by your boyfriend, nearly killed in an explosion and losing four members of your team?"

She turned her gaze toward the view and away from him. "I don't choose to dwell on the negative."

"That's understandable, Gennie, nobody likes to feel the pain."

She raised her glass to her lips and drained the merlot in one gulp, hoping to catch a buzz that would drown her other thoughts. Noah's comment was nothing new. She'd heard variations on the feel-your-pain theory from therapists, friends and family. They seemed to think that she couldn't truly heal unless she acknowledged the hurt.

They meant well, she knew that, but none of them understood her. They couldn't know that every day, sometimes every hour in the day, she thought of her team members who were killed in Afghanistan. Their deaths had wounded her deeply. She refused to forget those three men and one woman, even if it meant she'd never heal.

Noah had mentioned the injuries she'd suffered. Though she didn't want to go through that experience again, she didn't think her time in the hospital was bad luck. If anything, it was the opposite. She was blessed to have survived. Her physical limitations were better handled with therapy than with tears and moaning about how much she had suffered. Everybody hurts. She was glad she didn't have to feel all the pain.

Noah took a position on the balcony beside her. "More wine?"

"You don't know me," she said. "I can stick a pin in my leg and not experience the sensation, but I'll still bleed. Maybe I'm not weeping, but I have emotions."

"Tell me about Warrick."

Her guard went up. "What do you want to know?"

"Were you hurt when you suspected him of betrayal?"

"When he dumped me? Left me on a hospital bed? Never even called? Yeah, it hurt. But then I was angry, and I still am." She gestured with her wineglass, fighting an urge to hurl it off the balcony and see it shatter on the sidewalk far below. "Do we have to talk about him?"

"We do," he said. "Kenneth Warrick is the star player in this scenario. Even if he didn't kill Slocum, we need to figure out his motivations."

"I believe I would like more wine." She stalked back into the condo. In the sleek kitchen, she found the wine.

"You know him better than anybody," Noah said. "Why did he try to seduce Ruby?"

"I'm not so sure that he did." She poured herself more wine. "I've known Ruby for a long time. I like her and I believe that she loves Roger Haymarket with all her heart. But sometimes that lady plays fast and loose with the truth."

He poured himself another splash of merlot. "Why would she lie about Warrick?"

"Maybe she was and maybe she wasn't."

"Are you suggesting that there was another man, somebody else she kissed?"

"Not necessarily." Gennie drank deeply from her wineglass. It was entirely possible that Ruby had been momentarily swept off her feet by Warrick. Not only did he have a great body and striking blue eyes but he fired sexual sparks that ignited a woman's libido.

"At least, it wasn't Slocum. It's more believable that she was messing around with Warrick."

"Agreed," she said. "The only thing she and Slocum had in common, other than their shared fondness for the general, was a nose for gossip. The two of them could put their heads together and figure out who was sleeping around, who had plastic surgery and who had a gambling problem."

"Dangerous secrets," he said.

"They could be." Concentrating on the murder instead of her personal problems was a relief. Ruby had dropped a ton of information for them to investigate. "You mentioned blackmail."

"Gossip can be lucrative. Working as the aide to a four-star general, Slocum had access to a number of wealthy, powerful men who'd pay to keep their secrets private."

"That's what this is all about—secrets." He clinked his wineglass with hers, and they both took a drink. "I'll ask Anna Rose to use her cyber connections to verify Slocum's net worth. Over a million bucks plus properties?"

"That seems like an awful lot of money to make from blackmail."

"It depends on the wealth of the clients," he said. "Slocum might have been working his extortion schemes for years. I don't like to speak ill of the dead, but I can see Dean Slocum with his pressed trousers and his smooth platinum hair creeping around the edges of important conversations. Nobody would pay him much attention. They might even confide in him."

She went to the marble-topped island that separated the kitchen from the dining area and perched on a stool. From this position, she could see through the dining area into the front room with the fireplace. His neat, orderly condo made her aware of how much she wanted to clean up and get ready for bed. The black jumpsuit and cashmere vest she'd been wearing all night felt wilted and gross. "I need a shower."

"Maybe it's not blackmail at all."

"Then what?" she asked.

"Your old boyfriend has better ways to make big bucks. I'm talking illegal arms deals that Slocum could be brokering."

"I have a few problems with that scenario." Emphatically, she thrust her index finger in the air. "Number one—don't call that scumbag my boyfriend."

Noah gave a nod. "What's number two?"

"Warrick is greedy. If Slocum was his partner, there's

no way he'd share a million bucks." She paused for a moment to consider the possibilities. "On the other hand, the sale of illegal weapons is a vicious business. These are people who would think nothing of killing Slocum and Warrick and anybody else who got in their way."

"I'm glad you're not going to be alone tonight."

So am I. Though she had nothing to do with Warrick and whatever scheme he might be working, she might get caught in the crossfire by people who thought they were still connected. She knew better than to cross the warlords, cartels and criminals who trafficked in munitions. "Arms deals are complicated. There might be others involved."

"Do you have anybody in mind?"

A name popped to the forefront of her mind, but she placed her index finger across her lips to keep from blurting it out. The wine was beginning to loosen her tongue, and she didn't want to make a remark that she'd regret later.

Again, he asked, "Who?"

"Nobody." *Mitch Murano.* Though she had no tangible reason to suspect the Boulder guru, there was something about him that put her on edge.

"Tomorrow," he said. "We'll find out more when we go to the Haymarket mansion."

"Ruby said the general didn't want you there," she reminded him.

"I'll have to convince him that I can be useful."

Gennie anticipated a minor explosion from the general. He loved his wife and would do anything to please her, but he didn't like being pushed around. "Don't worry, Noah. If he boots you out, I can handle the situation by myself."

Though he didn't come right out and say that he didn't think she was capable of managing the general, Ruby and Slocum's next of kin, she could tell that he was doubtful. His forehead tensed, and he raked his fingers through his close-cropped hair.

She kept her gaze steady. They seemed to be teetering on the brink of an argument, and she wanted to be ready.

Instead of raising an objection, he finished his wine, set down the glass beside the sink and said, "We'll talk in the morning."

She followed him out of the kitchen and into the hallway that led to the bedrooms. "If things don't work out with the general, I'm sure you have a lot of business to take care of tomorrow."

"I should pay a visit to Murano at his institute," he said. "Zoey can come with me. Her insights might be useful. She hates that guy."

"But I want to go with you," she said quickly. "Warrick might be there. I should be the one who confronts him. Like you said, I know more about him than anybody else."

"But you're going to be busy at the general's house. You can't be in two places at once." He paused at the door to the guest bedroom where they had already dropped off her suitcase. "Sleep well, Gennie."

Her night with Noah hadn't turned out the way she'd hoped or expected. The attraction was there but so was the tension. The bed in the guest room tempted her with the promise of plump pillows and fresh linens.

But she needed a shower before she crawled under that crisp white duvet. Dragging herself across the room, she peeled off her clothes and kicked off her shoes. It took a moment to unwrap the ankle support, but when the pressure was relieved she was pleased. The swelling was almost gone, and she had a wide range of motion.

Inside the glass doors of the huge shower, she adjusted the faucets and ran her hand across a green tiled wall as she stepped into the spray. The water was screaming hot. Steam swirled around her arms and legs. The shower jets massaged her shoulders. Finally, she relaxed. The combination of wine and shower was better than a dozen sleeping pills and hours of meditation.

She looked forward to a peaceful night. No worries about tomorrow when she'd either be at the general's mansion or Murano's institute. Tonight, her mind would banish all thoughts of murderous arms cartels, smarmy blackmail schemes and how she could be attracted to Noah and annoyed with him at the same time.

Stepping from the shower, she toweled dry and took inventory of the pattern of light scars from the explosion in Afghanistan. After three years, most were barely noticeable. The worst was a shrapnel wound below her collarbone. The scar had bothered her enough that she'd disguised it with a tattoo of a butterfly. After she brushed her teeth, she slipped into a striped nightshirt and padded across the cashmere carpet toward the beautiful bed.

Her mouth was dry. Before she dove between the covers, she ought to get a glass of water from the kitchen. Also, she realized, she'd left her purse and cell phone on the counter. She eased open the door, hoping she wouldn't wake Noah, and tiptoed into the hall.

With the ambient light from the sliding-glass doors, she could see well enough to make her way down the hall. In the kitchen, she turned on the light over the stove and looked through a couple of cabinets for a water glass.

She heard him clear his throat. "Noah?"

"Can I help you with anything?"

He leaned against the doorjamb with his muscular arms folded across his naked chest. Plaid pajama bottoms hung from his hips. His dark brown hair was spiky from the shower. She didn't think he was purposely trying to be sexy but... Oh, my.

She swallowed hard. "Thirsty."

"Help yourself," he said. "I'm glad we ran into each other."

"Are you?" She filled her glass and took a gulp.

"When I said I wanted to go with you to the general's house, I didn't mean to imply that you couldn't handle questioning these people."

It was a legitimate concern. She wasn't trained as a detective. "I don't know much about interrogation."

"But you've got good instincts." He joined her at the sink and filled his own water glass. "You'll do fine."

His nearness—and his nakedness—were almost more than she could handle. His tanned chest seemed to glow in the dim light from above the stove. His arms were ripped but not bulky. If she stroked his flesh, she knew the skin would be supple and the muscles would be like steel. She felt herself leaning toward him. Her tight nipples were inches away from his chest. It was imperative for her to put distance between them.

"Phone," she blurted. "I came out here to check my cell phone."

Backing away from the sink, she grabbed her purse on the countertop and reached into the inner pocket where she kept her cell phone. "There's a text message from Ruby."

"No more trouble, I hope."

She read the text aloud: "Roger wants you to come for brunch at ten. It's okay to bring Noah."

"Practically an invitation," he said wryly.

There was no way to avoid spending more time with him tomorrow. Was she happy about this turn of events? She liked Noah. He was one of the good guys, maybe too good, definitely too appealing. When he moved toward her, she backed off again. "I should go to bed."

She fled down the hall to the guest bedroom. Her heart banged inside her rib cage. Any thoughts of a pleasant relaxing sleep were dead, but that wasn't an altogether bad thing. Sliding between the sheets, she smiled to herself. Tonight, she expected to have many hot, sensual dreams about Noah's bare chest.

Chapter Eleven

Five minutes before ten o'clock in the morning, Noah rang the doorbell at the entrance to the Haymarket mansion. Clad in a sports jacket, a necktie and a responsible attitude, he was ready for business. This meeting was an opportunity to mend ARC's relationship with the general, not to mention that he and Gennie could make progress on the murder investigation and shift the suspect spotlight off him.

He could tell that she was nervous. Her posture was as rigid as if she'd been standing at attention. He whispered, "It's going to be okay."

"Don't worry about me," she murmured under her breath. "I know how to keep my eyes open and my mouth shut."

The doorbell was answered by the housekeeper/butler. Henry Harrison was a slim gray-haired man who dressed in a black turtleneck, jeans and cowboy boots no matter what the season. He'd opted out of yesterday's event but returned to literally put the house in order. He gave Noah a quick hug and whispered, "I hear what they're saying, and they're wrong. I know you didn't kill him."

"Thanks, I think."

"But I wouldn't have blamed you too much if you did kill him. Captain Slocum was a hard man to get along with." He introduced himself to Gennie and escorted them down the hall to a sunny breakfast room where the general and Ruby sat at a round table, sipping coffee from bright yellow mugs. The cheerful decor and the vase of red and yellow tulips on the table contrasted the dark silence between husband and wife. Noah wondered if their mutual hostility was because she'd told him about the letter.

When the general shook his hand, he echoed Harrison's sentiment. "I don't consider you a suspect, Noah. But I'm damned angry about yesterday's security lapses."

"We could have done more." That was the only apology Noah was going to offer. According to the report he received this morning from Tony Vega, his field operatives performed their assignments as well as could have been expected. They hadn't prepared for such a well-planned, well-executed assault. The killer knew everything—from the range of the surveillance cameras to the best getaway route, and he'd used the crowds at the fund-raiser as cover. ARC Security hadn't made mistakes, but they hadn't anticipated the impossible.

Ruby came around the table, gave him and Gennie a hug and got them seated. After he took his first sip of Harrison's excellent coffee, Noah said, "I spoke to Anna Rose this morning, and she sends her condolences."

"I appreciate that." In his casual clothes and Broncos baseball cap, the general looked like he was more interested in eighteen holes of golf than in a murder investigation. "Anna Rose and I have known each other for a long time. Her husband was a good friend."

And she's an ace, brilliant cyber genius! Late last night, Noah had emailed her the information about Slocum's finances, and she'd already uncovered records to confirm the deceased man's worth at a million-plus. She'd also found addresses for two of his three properties. One was his primary residence in south Denver, and the other was near Boulder.

"Both Anna Rose and I had questions about the arrangements for the fund-raiser." Noah carefully kept his tone non-confrontational. "You requested twice the usual number of field operatives plus a sniper on the roof."

"That is correct."

"Did you have a reason to suspect there might be trouble?"

"Actually, Slocum was the one who suggested more security, which seemed odd because then he didn't want the metal detector at the door." The general scowled into his coffee mug. "In hindsight, I think he knew there might be danger and wanted extra protection."

"Who was the threat coming from?" Noah asked.

The general shook his head. "Don't know."

He sat back while Harrison and the cook served fruit cups, granola and an egg-white frittata casserole garnished with avocado. Noah was fairly sure that the general would have preferred bacon and grits, but other people—probably Ruby and the butler—were looking out for him, making sure he had a healthy breakfast. The general didn't sweat the small stuff, like a menu. Roger Haymarket had been a top-level military officer for decades. He was accustomed to having his basic needs taken care of and his orders obeyed.

"We should take a look at Mitch Murano," Gennie said as she filled her plate. "He's a public figure. Surely, he has enemies."

The general beamed at her across the table. "I'm so glad I can welcome you into my home. You were always special to me, Gennie, like the daughter I never had."

"Thank you, sir."

"A real Colorado gal," he said. He might joke around, but the general took his western heritage seriously. The Haymarket family was wealthy, powerful and owned thousands of acres of ranch land near Aspen. "I always bragged that you could shoot better, run faster and climb a sheer rock wall face without safety ropes. When you turned down a job working with me, I was real disappointed."

"All for the best," she said. "You wouldn't want me as an aide. I've got a temper."

"Well, you can be cantankerous." He turned to his wife. "Did I ever tell you that sweet little Gennie called me a bald-headed baboon?"

"Yes, you told me."

It seemed likely that the general had repeated that story dozens of times, and Gennie didn't appreciate the teasing. Her jaw tensed. An angry red flush crept up her throat.

The general dug into his fruit. "I'm hoping you and Ruby will start spending time together. You gals have a lot in common."

Did they? Noah glanced from Gennie in her simple olive green pantsuit with a sleeveless white top to

Ruby who wore full makeup, an armful of bracelets and a multicolored caftan. The differences between them went deeper than their clothing. Ruby was flamboyant and loved to gossip while Gennie kept her thoughts and feelings under tight control. Similarities? They were both determined and stubborn.

"Let's get back to Murano," Gennie said, stomping back into the conversation like a miniature Godzilla. "Are you aware that Kenneth Warrick is working for him under an alias?"

"The FBI investigators mentioned it. Before that, I didn't know. You've got to believe that if I had seen Warrick or heard his name, I would have told Mitch to fire him. Warrick is bad news. He was acquitted in our Afghanistan investigation, but I always thought he was involved in the staging of the explosion that nearly killed you."

"Have you spoken to Murano about him?"

"Not yet, I have a lot on my plate, sweetheart."

"When will you talk to him?"

"Well, aren't you a dog with a bone?" He reached over and patted her hand. "Don't worry, Gennie. I won't let Warrick get anywhere near you."

The blotchy red flush spread to her cheeks. Before Gennie erupted, Ruby redirected the conversation with light chatter about the delicious food. Noah was grateful. He couldn't excuse the general's condescending comments but didn't want to hurt the old man who seemed truly fond of Gennie.

Noah knew he was walking a delicate line with Gennie. He didn't want to say anything that would turn her against him, but he had to be cautious about his attraction that grew stronger by the minute. How could he be honest with her? Her direct approach with Haymarket wasn't a good way to get information from him, but he couldn't muzzle her.

Ruby checked her gold wristwatch. "Look at the time. Dean Slocum's next of kin will be arriving at any moment. Roger arranged for them to catch a military flight into Buckley. After they land, one of the men on base will drive them here."

Again, Noah was struck by the smooth efficiency of the general's life. It probably took one phone call to make those transportation arrangements. "I expect you'll miss Dean Slocum. It'll be difficult to find someone to fill Slocum's shoes."

"He was efficient," the general said. "An excellent factotum."

Gennie asked, "According to his sister-in-law, your factotum had over a million dollars in the bank. Do you have any idea how he came into so much money?"

He waggled a finger at her. "You've been talking to my wife, haven't you? She thinks Loretta Slocum is up to something. But I just don't believe it. Loretta and Buddy are salt-of-the-earth people with no hidden agendas and no underhanded plans."

"I hope you're right," Ruby said, exchanging a glance with him and with Gennie. "The FBI agents said that the next of kin are automatic suspects."

"Buddy and Loretta were in Nashville," her husband pointed out. "That's a damn solid alibi."

Ruby shot to her feet. "I'm going upstairs to change. Gennie, will you come with me?"

"You bet."

When the women left the breakfast room, the energy level dropped several degrees. Between the two of them, Ruby and Gennie used up a lot of oxygen. Noah looked over at the general. "They're something else, aren't they?"

"Gennie is still mad at me, but she'll come around."

Noah wasn't so sure about that. "It might take a while."

"Kenneth Warrick is a sore spot with her. That bastard didn't visit her in the hospital after she nearly died. She hates him, and I don't blame her. Frankly, I think the investigators got it wrong when they cleared him of all charges."

"You aren't the only one who had a problem with Warrick," Noah said. "Before the fund-raiser, Slocum told us to keep an eye out for him. That surprised me."

"Why's that?"

"Slocum and Warrick were birds of a feather. I could see them working together. Maybe they were partners."

"Makes sense, Warrick was an arms dealer." Like the military man he was, the general homed in on an idea and took action. He whipped out his cell phone, put through a call to his temporary aide and told him to contact another general in US Army Intelligence.

Noah wasn't sure that military intelligence would uncover the facts about illegal arms dealings quicker than Anna Rose with all her cyber connections. But the general appeared to be on his side. ARC was forgiven, and that was a goal he'd hoped to accomplish this morning.

Haymarket poured himself a second cup of coffee and added three sugars. "Did Slocum know that Warrick was working for Murano?"

"He was using an alias, but he wasn't in hiding. Gennie said that Warrick has changed his appearance."

"If he's still in the area, the FBI will find him."

Noah didn't share his confidence. In his experience, the feds tended to get tangled up in bureaucracy. "We'll see."

When they heard the front doorbell ring, both men rose from the breakfast table.

"That must be Buddy and Loretta." The general called out toward the kitchen. "Harrison, will you show our guests in here. And maybe you can rustle up some bacon. I wouldn't mind pancakes and maple syrup."

So much for fruit cups and frittatas, General Haymarket was in control.

GENNIE RECLINED ON a velvet sofa in Ruby's walk-in closet, which was as large as the master bedroom in her parents' house. The floor-to-ceiling racks of footwear displayed sneakers, pumps, stilettos and many, many boots. There were trays of jewelry, racks of scarves and shelves full of handbags. In addition to the gowns, day dresses and suits, Ruby owned a huge collection of Western clothing with elaborate embroidery and miles of fringe.

As she tried on outfits, she narrated each of her choices. "This full skirt shows that I'm sweet and feminine. And I'll go with flat-heeled pumps in case Loretta is short. I don't want to tower over her. These pearls are a nice touch. What do you think?"

"You look like a 1950s housewife."

"Perfect! That's non-threatening and approachable." *And maybe a little bit weird.* "I liked the black leather biker chick outfit. Dressed like that, you could get tough with Loretta and make demands."

Ruby pointed a manicured black fingernail at her. "That's going to be your role. You'll be the bad cop, and I'll be the good cop."

Gennie lacked experience in interrogation techniques and didn't want to get complicated. "Role playing? I don't think so."

"Come on, it'll be fun." She flounced and preened in front of the full-length mirror. "I'll tell the sister-in-law that we want to help her, and you can scare her with threats about what's going to happen if she doesn't turn over that letter."

"I'm not the bad cop."

"Really?"

"And this isn't a game." Gennie had never been a girlie girl who liked to dress up and parade around. She stood and went to the window—amazed that there was actually a window in the closet. "Dean Slocum was murdered, and the killer is still out there. We can't ignore the danger."

"Oooh, that's good. You'll scare the Spanks off Loretta."

Harrison tapped on the door. "Are you decent? Mrs. Slocum wants to talk to you."

A shiver trembled across Ruby's shoulders, and Gennie was glad to see that glimmer of fear. Ruby wasn't an airhead. She knew there was danger. "What should I do?"

"Tell Harrison to escort her into the closet," Gennie advised. "One look at this wardrobe and she'll be stunned into silence."

When the angry little woman from Tennessee came into the room, she was the opposite of silent. Instead, she belted out an *OMG*, which was followed by a series of *oohs* and *aahs* as she circled the closet, greeting the designer clothes and shoes by name—Dior, Louboutin, St. Laurent, Prada—as though they were old friends. Her rapid tour came to an end in front of Ruby.

Shoving her curly brown perm off her forehead, Loretta stamped her foot, sending a jiggle through her plump body. Her blue eyes fired daggers and her lips twisted in a scowl. "I was right about you, Ruby. You are a *bona fide* gold digger."

"Good point," Gennie said, stepping forward. "When Ruby married the general, she struck it rich. Look around this closet. It's a treasure trove. And you know what that means?"

"What?" Loretta demanded.

"Ruby wasn't after your brother-in-law's money. She's got plenty of her own."

"But she kissed him."

"No, I did not," Ruby said. "I was never attracted to Dean, not in the least."

"Understandable," Loretta said with a smug grin. "Dean got the smarts in the family, and my husband is the handsome one. Buddy is taller and doesn't look like an albino freak show."

Gennie winced at the description. Loretta didn't have much affection for her brother-in-law. And yet, he'd sent her that letter, which could be used for blackmail. Were Loretta and Buddy working as partners? Turning that idea over in her mind, Gennie tried to think of a way to ease into the topic.

Ruby had distracted Loretta with shoes. Though there was a six-inch difference in their height, they both wore size seven and a half. Sitting on a velvet bench, Loretta tried on a pair of silver platform sandals with an ankle strap. She stood and strutted. The silver matched a stripe on the black leather purse slung across her shoulder, and the shoes actually looked good paired with the black leggings she wore under a flowered tunic.

"Those are perfect for you. I want you to have them," Ruby said. "Maybe we can make a trade. You have something I want."

"Aren't you the sweetest thing? But you can't buy me off with a pair of secondhand sandals even if they look like they were custom made for my feet." Like a magpie searching for shiny objects, Loretta fluttered around the closet until she found the pullout shelves filled with costume jewelry. "A silver necklace might be nice or pearls like the ones you're wearing."

Gennie had the feeling that this fashion show could drag on forever. She'd run out of patience. "Sit down, Loretta. We need to talk."

"You have no call to be rude."

"Sit." Gennie stood over Loretta and waited until she lowered her bottom onto one of the velvet benches. "Pay attention. This is something you need to hear."

"Fine."

"I was one of the first people who discovered Dean's body in the library. The first thing I saw was blood. He was sprawled back on the sofa, staring at the ceiling with dead eyes. He'd been stabbed in the chest with a double-edged blade, but he didn't die right away. He struggled, tried to run, tried to fight back. Blood was everywhere, streaks of it colored his face and matted in his hair. And then, the killer slashed his throat. Unable to call for help, he drowned in his own blood. Not an easy death."

Both women stared at her wide-eyed.

"Why are you telling me this?" Loretta asked in a tiny voice.

"The killer might strike again. You need to be careful, both of you."

"I didn't do anything wrong," Loretta said.

"The killer might see it differently," Gennie explained. "He or she might think you were involved. If you weren't, why did Dean send you that letter?"

"Maybe he was proud of himself for nailing the general's wife."

"Nobody nailed me," Ruby snapped.

Gennie stood over the short round woman from Nashville, blocking her escape. "Did Dean send you anything else, like other letters or photos or recordings?"

"Maybe he did." Her gaze darted. "I never did anything with the stuff he sent. I barely even looked at it."

If Dean Slocum was running an extortion scam, which Gennie thought was likely, he might have been using his sister-in-law as an insurance policy. He'd tell the people he was blackmailing that he had the evidence hidden in a safe place, and it would only be exposed if he was hurt or injured. If that was the case, Loretta was in deep, deep trouble.

"Did you bring the things Dean sent with you?"

"Sure did, but they're not the originals." Loretta dug into her purse with the silver stripe and pulled out a powder blue cell phone. "It's all in here."

"My letter," Ruby said. "Do you have it in there?"

"Just a copy," Loretta explained. "Dean bought me this nice phone about a year ago. Every once in a while, he'd send me documents in a closed file for safekeeping."

"But you figured out how to open the files," Gennie guessed.

"There are some really gross photos. You wouldn't believe the sick, ugly things people do to each other."

"You need to turn your phone over to the FBI."

"Wait," Ruby said. "Maybe she should hold on to her phone."

Gennie could see the two of them forming an alliance. Ruby would go to great lengths to keep the letter away from her husband, and Loretta sensed opportunity. She wanted her chance to get rich like her blackmailing brother-in-law.

"You're in danger," Gennie said, loud and clear.

Loretta stood and sidled closer to Ruby. "The way I see it, the files on my phone mean nothing. Dean must have hidden the originals. It's worth checking his house."

"I'll drive," Ruby said.

"Bad idea," Gennie said as she blocked the exit. "You could be murdered."

"That's why you're coming along," Ruby said. "Gennie, you're my bodyguard."

She and Loretta were already marching out the door. Gennie had no choice. She had to protect these two crazy ladies.

Chapter Twelve

Gennie wished she'd been more convincing as the "bad cop." She should have been tough and kickass. Should have drawn her Beretta, forced Ruby to back down and shot Loretta in her shiny new silver sandals. Instead, she was riding in the back seat of a luxury SUV while Ruby drove and Loretta sat in the passenger seat and schemed.

The best Gennie could hope for was to minimize the damage. She'd already taken a strategic precaution—something she hoped Loretta wouldn't notice.

"I never should have written that letter," Ruby said.

"If it wasn't about Dean," Loretta said, "who was the guy?"

"His name is Kenneth Warrick. He's a hot, sexy bad boy. All I did was kiss him, nothing else."

"Was he worth it?" Loretta asked slyly.

"Not even close. No other man compares to my husband. I don't know what came over me. Warrick is seductive in a creepy way. You can ask Gennie. She was engaged to him."

Loretta peeked around the passenger seat to look at her. "You?"

"It was long ago, another lifetime."

"But now you're falling for that Noah Sheridan. Am I right?"

"He's my boss." She pressed her back into the smooth leather seat, wanting to disappear. When Noah found out what she'd done, he'd be furious. She wouldn't blame him if he fired her. Using her cell phone, she sent him a text, outlining their plan to visit Dean's house in south Denver and then return to the mansion.

"Once we get there," Loretta said, "we'll go in different directions to search for the originals. The actual stuff Dean sent me was six letters, seventy-two email transcripts, a handful of receipts and twenty-seven photos—enough to fill a legal-size manila envelope. But you should keep in mind that we might be looking for something tiny, like the key to a safe deposit box."

"If we find this stuff," Ruby said, "what are we going to do with it?"

Loretta answered quickly. "Not blackmail, I won't do anything illegal. But there are media outlets that pay for these kinds of stories. And I just happen to have a podcast of my very own. I can use this dirt from Dean to further my journalistic career."

"Like a gossip reporter," Ruby said.

"Exactly, I could get my own reality show."

Gennie groaned. The Loretta Slocum Show was a scary thought.

"Here's something I don't understand," Ruby said. "Why didn't Dean leave these documents with his attorney?"

Loretta shrugged. "Maybe he didn't trust the guy."

"Have you talked to the lawyer? Do you know what you're going to inherit?"

"Dean's will was simple and straightforward. Except for a couple of stipends to special friends, the whole inheritance—the cash and the property—goes to Buddy."

"Whoa," Gennie said, pulling back on invisible reins. "This doesn't make sense, Loretta. You're already rich. Why mess around with Dean's dirty little secrets?"

"It's the principle of the thing. I could be rich…and famous, too."

"If you had a reality show," Ruby said, "I'd watch."

Don't encourage her. "What does Buddy think of your plan?"

"The big lug is okay with anything I do. He's no genius, but he's not stupid. In fact, he's one of the best mechanics in Nashville." She ran her fingers along the console of Ruby's luxury SUV. "He handles a lot of high-end vehicles like this one. He's shown me how to make repairs and adjustments in case I ever run into car trouble."

Following the GPS directions, Ruby took a right turn onto a pleasant street where mature trees shaded the sidewalks. Most of the houses had white or beige siding and were more modern in design than Gennie's north Denver neighborhood. Dean's address was the second from the corner on the right—a one-story beige brick with a small covered porch. The moment the SUV parked, Loretta flung her door open and charged toward the front door, moving at a surprising rate of speed for someone wearing platform sandals.

"Wait," Gennie called after her. Hadn't Loretta been

listening to the warnings about bloody murder and danger? "You need to be careful."

"It's all right," Loretta said with a wave. "I have a key."

"Stay close to me," Gennie instructed Ruby. She vaulted across the lawn, caught up with Loretta on the porch, grasped her arm and held her against the wall beside the mailbox.

"What are you doing?" Loretta demanded.

"My job," Gennie said. "Neither of you are going to get killed on my watch. That means I enter the house first and make sure there's nothing dangerous inside."

"You heard her," Ruby said.

With an angry flounce, Loretta stepped away from the door.

Gennie took her Beretta from the holster. Her instincts told her that something was wrong—nothing she could clearly identify but there was a stink of danger that reminded her of military exercises in Afghanistan. She wasn't going to like whatever was inside this house.

Trying to pinpoint the threat, she listened intently. It was totally quiet. There were no birds or squirrels in the trees. The blinds were drawn so she couldn't see inside. When she opened the screen door, she noticed that the painted gray door was slightly ajar.

She glanced over her shoulder at the other two women. "Wait here."

Before Loretta could whine and make objections, Gennie shoved the door open and rushed inside with her Beretta held in both hands, ready to aim and fire. The house felt empty, desolate and ruined. It had been trashed. Furniture was overturned, papers scattered and books pulled from their shelves.

She made a quick circuit of the living room, dining room and kitchen where the contents of the refrigerator were strewn on the tile floor and every cabinet door hung open. She returned to the front door where she motioned for Ruby and Loretta to come inside. "Stay by the door and be quiet while I make sure the rest of the house is clear."

"I have a gun," Ruby said.

"What?"

"I stuck it in my purse before we left the house."

"Leave it in your purse." She hurried down the hall, checked out the bathroom and bedrooms and came back to Ruby and Loretta. "Whoever did this is gone."

Loretta had taken Ruby's gun. She brandished the weapon as she stalked through the house. In the living room, she snatched a sofa cushion that had been slashed open. "This is my inheritance. Why would somebody do this to me?"

"I doubt it was personal," Gennie said. "Not unless they'd met you."

Ruby trembled, obviously shaken. "They were looking for evidence. Just like us."

Loretta came back and stood before them. "Now what? How can we tell if they found what they were looking for?"

"We can't," Gennie said as she took out her cell phone. "Conventional wisdom says that a search will cease as soon as the object is located. Since I see no sign of this quest ending, I'd guess that they weren't successful."

"Dean owned two other properties. We need to go to those." Loretta pivoted and scanned the torn apart room. "First, we should make sure it's not here."

"But we're not going to do any searching," Gennie said. "I'm calling the FBI."

"Why?"

"This is a crime scene. They have forensic investigators who can find clues to identify the person who did this."

"I can't take any more." With a little sob, Ruby leaned against the wall by the door. "I need to sit down."

In spite of her exquisite makeup, she looked pale and exhausted. Though Gennie knew they shouldn't touch anything and leave fingerprints, she directed Ruby to the dining room table and found a chair where she could rest and catch her breath.

"It's going to be all right," Gennie said.

"I should have told Roger. He'll forgive me, won't he?" There was a catch in her voice. "He has to forgive me. I can't live without him."

Gennie wished she could offer reassurance. She'd always felt that the cornerstone of any relationship was trust, and you can't believe in someone if they're lying. Her blunt, direct style hadn't always served her well, which might be why she was alone. "You owe your husband the truth."

"He's a good man." She clutched Gennie's hand. "He really wants the best for you."

Gennie heard the subtle beep from a luxury SUV. She looked for Loretta. The small woman from Tennessee was nowhere in sight. Gennie and Ruby got to the front door in time to see Loretta wave from the driver's seat and pull away from the curb.

"What the hell?" Ruby's malaise was eclipsed by her anger. "The bitch is stealing my car."

"When she took your gun from your purse, she must have grabbed the ignition fob."

"She won't get away with this," Ruby said. "My SUV has a tracking system. We'll know exactly where she is."

"Or she could disable that system." Hadn't Loretta told them that she knew how to make adjustments to luxury cars? "It's time for me to call the FBI."

Maybe the federal agents would have more luck in controlling a greedy little woman in silver shoes.

NOAH HAD ACCOMPLISHED his number one goal: establishing renewed trust with the general. They became allies when Haymarket started considering the potential military ramifications—especially arms smuggling—of Dean Slocum's murder. As soon as the general discovered that his wife and Loretta had taken off, he wanted to hire a couple of full-time bodyguards from ARC. Immediately, Noah set those wheels in motion. That was the good news.

The bad news was Gennie. For some unknown reason, she'd allowed herself to be drawn into what sounded like a lunatic scheme at Slocum's south Denver house. Making things worse, Loretta had stolen Ruby's car and disconnected the tracking system so she couldn't be traced.

Sitting rigid in the passenger seat of his SUV, Gennie stared through the windshield. There was no need to scold her. Regret and frustration swirled around her, but she hadn't fallen apart. While the general and the feds questioned her—she remained stoic, taking their criticism without flinching.

"Let me get this straight," he said. "How did Loretta get her hands on a gun?"

"It belonged to Ruby who stuck it in her purse before we left the house. Have you ever seen her closet?"

"Not my thing."

"It's huge with a zillion shoes and outfits, all with accessories to match. I think her gun falls into that category. It's something she carries when it's chic to be armed."

The description sounded exactly like Ruby—flashy, flamboyant and not very practical. Still, he liked her and the general, too. Noah was glad to have them back on the roster of ARC clients. He'd already assigned bodyguard duties to Greg and Zoey, as well as Tony Vega who was becoming an indispensable part of his operations. Noah had no problem with leaving Tony in charge while he pursued another avenue of investigation. He and Gennie were on their way to Boulder and had almost reached their destination. Afternoon sunlight highlighted the Flatirons west of town.

"When we get to MIME," he said as he exited the highway, "we need a strategy to talk to Murano."

"He's not the killer," she said. "I should know because I'm his alibi."

"But he's in the middle of all these different pieces. He's the general's golf buddy, and he had an altercation with Ruby. Also, Kenneth Warrick works for him. That's our secondary objective—find Warrick and question him."

"He's already pulled a disappearing act. The feds have been searching for him all over the place, and they've come up empty."

"We've got an advantage." He reached across the seats and touched her shoulder. "We've got you."

"Me?"

"Warrick sent you two messages. He did that weird thing with the flowers that he knew you'd understand. And he made an actual physical appearance in the ball-room. As far as we know, you were the only person who noticed him."

"He's taunting me." Her gaze hardened. She probably thought she was coming across as fierce, but he was momentarily mesmerized by the bright blue of her eyes. She cleared her throat and continued, "He wants to make me feel bad, to show me that he's so much smarter than I am."

He recalibrated his focus. No matter how much he wanted to reassure her, he had to treat her like a colleague. "Do you think he killed Slocum?"

"I wouldn't be surprised." She hesitated. "The complicated plotting and strange getaway seem like things Warrick would do. He'd get a kick out of outsmarting the FBI."

"But you have doubts about his guilt."

"When I was in the hospital, recovering from my injuries, I had a lot of time to consider my feelings about that man. I spent days blaming myself, thinking that I should have known him better and then I could have prevented the explosion. Not true! I wasn't responsible for his actions and couldn't take anything he did personally. Warrick is motivated by two things—money and power. If he thought he had something to gain from killing Slocum, he'd do it."

He appreciated her insight. "Why be so dramatic about the murder?"

"Ego," she said.

Anna Rose had said something similar. "Explain."

"He's a showboat. If he committed the murder, you can bet that he's staying nearby so he can watch everybody running around and investigating. He's probably laughing his ass off."

The idea of Warrick thinking for one minute that he'd bested ARC, local law enforcement and the FBI enraged him. Noah was beginning to take this investigation personally. "The general and I were talking about the power angle. Warrick might be involved in arms smuggling. If Slocum found out and tried to blackmail him, that makes a neat motive for murder."

An incongruous grin stretched her wide mouth. "Lucky for us, I have a way to prove or disprove that theory."

"What's that?"

She waved a blue cell phone at him. "This is the magical key that unlocks Dean Slocum's secrets. He sent his blackmail photos, letters and receipts to this phone that belongs to Loretta. I swiped it from her purse."

He was glad to have this advantage but surprised that she hadn't followed the rules. "How come you didn't hand this evidence over to the FBI?"

"If the feds had asked for the phone, I would have given it to them. But they were too busy being condescending to me. I really disliked the guy who kept twirling his pen between his fingers like a miniature baton, acting as though I didn't deserve his full attention. I wanted to grab his ballpoint, stab it into his thigh and watch him bleed."

"You've got a dark side, Gennie."

"Is that a problem?"

What had he expected? During the exercise at his cabin, she'd picked the lock, slaughtered the guys who were posing as guards and bested him in hand-to-hand combat. "No problem at all."

"I'm a rational person. I was trained as a soldier, and my first loyalty is to the people who care about me. In this situation, that's ARC."

"Do you know how to unlock her phone?"

"Nope."

"Call Anna Rose. She'll figure it out."

While Gennie made the call and fiddled with the electronics, he concentrated on the GPS instructions that would lead them to Murano's institute in the mountains outside of town. Following a paved two-lane road, they crossed a wide field where bright red and blue wildflowers were starting to appear. Gennie probably knew their names and meanings and could use them to predict the future or make tea. After the field, he drove into a forest.

"That does it," she said as she finished her call. "Loretta's phone is unlocked and I've sent copies of the files to Anna Rose. Do you think we should read a couple? I'm curious to see the letter from Ruby."

"Let's wait until after we're done at MIME." He wanted her to focus on what they were about to face. "Warrick will have to make contact with you."

"That won't happen unless he thinks he's alone with me."

That was the obvious flaw in his plan. He wanted

to use Gennie as bait, but he couldn't risk leaving her vulnerable. "Too dangerous."

"I'm armed and can protect myself," she said coolly. "If it makes you feel better, I can put in my earbud and microphone."

Noah still wasn't crazy about the idea, but he couldn't think of any other way. "If you need backup, don't hesitate to call out. I'll stay close."

"And I'll be careful."

Her casual promise didn't reassure him, but he'd spent the past week watching her train and practice marksmanship. He had to trust her. "Try to get him to say something incriminating."

"How do I do that?"

"I don't know. Use your feminine wiles."

She scoffed. "I've never found my wiles to be useful. It might be better if I break his nose or shoot off a kneecap. I have that dark side, remember?"

"Please take this seriously, Gennie. Warrick could be dangerous."

When the SUV emerged from the forest, they had a view of Murano's Institute. In the distance, he saw a massive stone lodge. Farther up the hillside were several A-frame cottages.

"Murano might be a jerk," she said. "But this place is spectacular. It reminds me of Oz."

"And we're going to see the wizard."

Chapter Thirteen

Noah didn't know much about Murano's philosophy, but the guru must have been doing something right. MIME was obviously a high-end operation. The fields, hillsides, creeks and forests that made up the grounds were prime real estate that had been developed with care, enhancing the indigenous rocks and trees. The centerpiece was a four-story lodge built from cedar and natural stone. Seven chimneys protruded from the roof. At the south end was a square tower with an open cupola on the top.

At the entrance, Noah waved off the valet and parked the SUV himself. He wanted to be prepared if they needed to make a quick exit. The parking area was at the north end of the lodge. This vantage point overlooked a large swimming pool built into the surrounding rocks.

Gennie stared down at the rippling water with wisps of steam rising from it. "Do you think it's heated by a hot spring?"

"There are a lot of thermal pools in the area, some of them are mineral rich and supposedly therapeutic."

"I'd love to take a swim."

"Me, too." If they hadn't been here investigating a

murder, they could have stripped down and slid into the warm caress of a natural hot spring pool. He couldn't stop his imagination from picturing her as a water sprite, naked and wet and beautiful.

"I wouldn't mind signing up for a long weekend of soaking," she said. "There are probably spa treatments and a masseuse."

"And a gourmet restaurant that features certified organic ingredients. Murano's chef provided some of the canapés for the fund-raiser, and they were great." He shrugged. "I guess you could say that this is the first-class pass to Nirvana."

"Fine with me," she said. "I've always preferred luxury to self-flagellation and fasting."

While Noah thought of the many ways he'd like to pamper her, they hiked to the house and climbed the four stairs to a stone veranda that stretched across the front. There weren't many people around. The four who sat in carved wood chairs on the veranda smiled, nodded and went back to their afternoon relaxation. Inside, Noah and Gennie were greeted in the vast, open lobby by an attractive blond woman wearing moccasins, a long skirt and lots of turquoise jewelry.

When he asked her how many people were staying here, she told him that they were at 80 percent capacity in the lodge and all the private cabins were occupied. This afternoon, most of the patrons were in a lecture hall, listening to a renowned astrophysicist discuss the role of the stars and planets in everyday life. She ushered them into a waiting room, served them bottled water from a small refrigerator and told them that Dr. Murano would be with them shortly.

A giant TV hung on the wall opposite the south-western-style sofa. The high-resolution screen showed continuous images touting MIME. Gennie leaned back on the sofa, sipped her water and subtly scanned the plants, the decorative glasswork on the side tables and the casual decor. Looking for hidden surveillance cameras? That was exactly what he'd done when he walked through the door. Though he hadn't spotted the telltale glint of a lens, he assumed they were being watched.

She picked up a remote from a coffee table and activated the sound that went with the screen images. "Do you mind?" she asked. "I'm curious about what happens here."

"You're just looking for a reason to hang out at the hot springs."

"Yes, please."

The image on the screen showed a Native American sweat lodge that looked like a flat-topped tipi made of canvas and bent branches with heated stones inside. The narrator discussed how several tribes used the sweat lodge to expand their consciousness and compared their ritual to sauna and hot yoga. The Murano version of enlightenment included bits and pieces from many other theories, religions and lifestyles, which the narrator called "global stimulation and awareness." Noah thought the Institute's philosophy fit into the category of "whatever feels good." Fine with him, he didn't judge. If rich people wanted to throw their money away on a slick con man, that was their right. The scary part was that Mitch Murano had a good shot at becoming the next state senator from Colorado.

Murano swept into the room and rushed toward them

in a burst of enthusiasm that had to be phony. Why would he be thrilled to meet them again? His shoulder-length black hair swirled around his high cheekbones. His loose white linen shirt emphasized his healthy tan.

With a two-handed grip, he clasped Gennie's hand. "So good to see you. I'll enjoy showing you around."

"I like what I saw of your pool," she said.

"The hot springs are extensive. Several of them flow through underground grottoes with mysterious, glowing rocks." He turned toward Noah and gently patted his shoulder. "You're doing well. I'm glad you're already up and around after what happened."

Noah took offense to being treated like a victim. Murano's comment made him feel like less of a man. "My injuries were minor."

"But you were unconscious."

"I was drugged." He didn't yet have the official results back, but he knew what had happened. He was hit twice by a stun gun and doped up. "The dose wore off, and I was fine."

"Still," Murano said, "it must have been traumatic."

His words sounded sensitive but there was a condescending sneer behind them. He reminded Noah of how Gennie felt about the FBI agent with the twirling pen. Noah curbed his hostility. There was no point in alienating a potential witness.

Gennie pointed to the ongoing narrative on the TV where an array of jewelry, glass bowls and sculptures were displayed. "That's your family, right? You're descended from the people in Italy who make Murano glass like the vase over there and the bowl on the table."

"Distantly related." He used the remote to turn off

the TV. "My roots have been in America for six generations, but I reconnected with the family in Italy and did some importing before I discovered my true calling."

"Meditation and enlightenment," Noah said. "Where did you get your training?"

"My MA is from Naropa, right here in Boulder, and my doctorate from Berkeley. I've studied at many other learning institutions, but most of my work is intuitive. I tailor each program to the specific needs of the client."

"Zoey Potter," Gennie said. "What program did you use with her?"

He raked his fingers through his long thick hair, dragging it off his forehead. He frowned. "I don't remember her."

"What about Ruby Haymarket?"

Noah appreciated Gennie's blunt interrogation. If he'd asked those questions, he would have come off as being aggressive. She could get away with borderline rudeness because her blond hair and big blue eyes made her appear sweet and innocent. He smiled to himself, remembering her dark side—a deep intriguing secret.

"Ruby doesn't like you very much," Gennie said. "Why is that?"

"We never found common ground," he admitted. "All she wanted from me was a weight-loss program. I was sorry it didn't work out because Roger and I got along so well, and he was concerned about his wife. I had hoped to set up a couples' meditation for them, to enhance their relationship."

"Couples' meditation," Noah said. Some of Murano's ideas were intriguing, might as well try to give him the benefit of the doubt. "How does that work?"

"It's based on Kundalini yoga meditations and exercises to open the root chakra in order to get in touch with your sensual energy."

"Sounds sexy," Gennie said.

"It's powerful but not for everybody," Murano said.

"Give me an example," she said.

"Let us suppose for a moment that you and Noah are a couple. I can evaluate your ability to join together and bond by asking one simple question. You must answer simultaneously."

"Okay," she said. "Ask."

"What is the most important factor in a relationship?"

Noah only needed a second to respond. "It's love."

"Trust," she said just as quickly.

Murano gestured like a magician who had just pulled a rabbit out of his hat. "And that, my friends, is why you are not a couple and never will be. Noah's natural power and energy arises from his fourth chakra, his heart. Gennie's strength comes from a more logical and thoughtful place, possibly focused on the sixth chakra, the third eye."

They'd never be a couple? Noah's momentary good will toward Murano vanished. He felt like picking up the leaded glass bowl on the table and beating him over the head with it. The time had come to get down to business. "We came here to ask you a few questions about one of your employees."

"The man you call Kenneth Warrick." Murano paced across the room and adjusted the position of a pear-shaped vase on a table. Though he didn't appear agitated, his attitude was a few degrees less smug. "I won't be much help. We've met but I barely know the man. I have over three hundred employees, including the part-timers."

"Really," Gennie said. "This is a bigger operation than I thought."

"The operation of the lodge and restaurant is equivalent to running a small hotel, and this isn't my only location. I maintain an office in town to handle my contacts, publications and lectures to promote my programs. Ever since I stepped into the political arena, my workload has expanded exponentially. I've needed to hire new people."

Noah asked, "Did you interview Warrick before he joined your security detail?"

"I did not," he said. "The man in charge of security does the interviewing and hiring."

"Were you familiar with Warrick's history in Afghanistan or his prior relationship with General Haymarket?"

"The FBI asked these same questions," Murano said.

Noah picked up on the fact that Murano hadn't actually given him an answer. While he'd been talking about himself and his accomplishments, his replies sounded glib and direct, almost rehearsed. Talking about Warrick wasn't so clear-cut.

There was something the guru wasn't telling them, something he wanted to hide. Was it about Afghanistan or the general or both? Noah took a shot. "Ruby Haymarket recognized Warrick. Did she tell you?"

"Ruby said a great many things."

Again, he didn't answer. Murano was going to be a great politician. He'd already developed the tactic of dodging the truth. Noah pressed forward. "Dean Slocum was an extortionist. Did he ever approach you?"

"Are you accusing me of a crime?"

"The opposite," Noah said. "I'm suggesting that you might have been blackmailed. You were the victim."

"In the first place, I've done nothing wrong. My life is an open book." He flashed his whitened smile. "If Captain Slocum had tried to blackmail me, don't you think I would have reported him to the authorities? I'm running for senator. I can't afford some ridiculous blackmail threat."

"I understand," Noah said.

Still smiling, Mitch Murano gestured for them to follow him for a grand tour of the Institute. For a guy who was supposed to be intuitive, he wasn't really on his toes. When he said he couldn't afford to be blackmailed, he'd given himself a motive for murder.

As soon as they got the chance, he and Gennie needed to search through the evidence that Slocum had stored on Loretta's cell phone.

STANDING IN THE open cupola atop the stone tower at the north end of the lodge, Gennie thought of the minarets in Kabul. That city was half a world away from the Rocky Mountains, but her memories brought Afghanistan close. Remembered echoes from the minaret—the call to prayer—reverberated inside her head. Her nose itched with the remembered smell of the dirt and the gunpowder that always seemed to hang in the air. In that rugged terrain, her life had been forever altered. Central to that change was Kenneth Warrick.

She was anxious to confront him and find out how

he was involved in the murder. If that happened, if they met, she would not fail. During the investigation three years ago, he'd talked his way out of trouble. Not this time.

Murano lightly touched her shoulder. "In a place of such beauty, meditation becomes second nature."

"It's very peaceful," she said, though she wasn't feeling serene at all.

"Rainclouds are coming in from the north," Noah said. He'd taken off his sports jacket and rolled up the sleeves on his oxford blue shirt. A crisp breeze ruffled the light brown hair on his forearms. "April showers, right?"

"We need the moisture," Murano said, echoing the typical refrain from Coloradoans. "It's good as long as it doesn't turn into flash floods."

Listening to a weather report wasn't getting her any closer to her goal. She had to find a way to escape from these two men without being obvious. Murano had insisted on shepherding them around.

Noah commented, "The tower seems older than the rest of the lodge."

"Good observation. The original structure was built in 1902 by a family of Scottish ranchers. In 1989, a local developer bought the property and started renovations. I've owned the Institute since I was forty, almost fourteen years ago. When I bought it, I thought it would be a grand legacy."

"I didn't know you had children," she said.

"I don't," he said. "The world is my legacy."

She scanned from left to right—from the hot spring pool to the small private cabins to the trailheads for hiking excursions. Employees in dark blue polo shirts bustled from one spot to another. The few patrons who weren't attending the astrophysics lecture dressed in loose linen shirts like Murano. They meandered around the grounds with less sense of purpose. She studied each person, looking for Warrick.

"Deeper in the forest," he said, "there are mini-villages of tipis and sweat lodges."

She pointed. "Is that a newly planted vegetable garden?"

"Good eye, Gennie. That small plot is right outside our restaurant and dining hall. As I'm sure you know, our arid climate and rocky soil in the mountains are limitations, but my chef is determined to grow our own produce. He likes to experiment."

Noah asked, "How much do you know about plants?"

"Not as much as I'd like," Murano responded.

"Gennie is kind of an expert on growing herbs and vegetables in difficult climates, like Afghanistan. Maybe she could give your chef a few pointers."

Immediately, she perked up. Noah was handing her an excuse to break away from them and find Warrick. She snatched the opportunity. "I'd love to talk to your gardeners."

"Of course," Murano said.

Before he could change his mind, Noah said, "If you don't mind, I'd very much like to see your collection of glass. Gennie, why don't you check out the garden by yourself?"

Behind Murano's back, he mouthed the words, "Be careful."

She bobbed her head and looked away, surprised by

the sudden warmth that arose inside her. Noah's concern for her safety was unnecessary but touching. For half a second, she wished she was the type of woman who needed his protection—a fairy princess who could swoon into his muscular arms. Instead, she was capable of slaying her own dragons.

"We'll meet on the veranda," she said, "in a half hour or forty-five minutes."

She was off, dashing down the enclosed staircase rather than using the slow elevator that must have been installed when the lodge was built in 1902. She needed to move, to get her blood circulating. Since it was close to dinnertime and the kitchen staff would be busy, she figured that she didn't need to put in an appearance at the kitchen. Her excuse would be that she didn't want to interrupt.

When she reached the lower level, she paused to insert her earbud and activate her microphone so that she could communicate with Noah. She whispered into the mic, "If you can hear me, ask Murano when the lecture will be over."

Through her earbud, she heard him pose the question. Noah repeated Murano's answer. The lecture would be over in twenty minutes. She didn't have much time to make contact with Warrick before the patrons of MIME swarmed the grounds.

She pushed open a heavy wooden door and stepped outside. If Warrick was here, she figured that he'd be holed up inside the lodge, peering out through a window and staying hidden from the FBI and local law enforcement. The best way to lure him out was to show herself and let him know she was alone. On a paved pathway behind the lodge, she walked toward the pool. Waving at the lodge was probably too aggressive, but she stared at each floor and each window.

Concentrating, she sent a mental message. *Come out, come out, wherever you are.* If he was here, he'd approach her. Warrick was egotistical enough to believe that she'd forgiven him and was desperate to see him after catching a glimpse at the fund-raiser.

Too quickly, she reached the edge of the pool. The minutes were slipping away. A small tasteful sign advised that swimming was prohibited when there was no lifeguard on duty, but she still found it odd that there was no one in the water. This was, by far, the most appealing feature of MIME, but nobody was here. *Come on, Warrick, find me. I'm waiting.*

A gentle breeze twirled the rising steam in a delicate pirouette across the surface of the water. She knelt on the rugged stones at the edge, peeled off her jacket and leaned down to trail her hand and arm in the water. Warm as a bathtub, the liquid soothed her so much that she almost forgot her mission. A low groan pushed through her lips.

"I remember that sound. You used to moan like that in bed."

She sprang to her feet, drew her Beretta and aimed the barrel at Kenneth Warrick's gut. "Where did you come from?"

"I've been keeping tabs on you since you got here." He showed her his hands. "I'm unarmed. You can put that gun away."

Her trigger finger twitched. She thought of the men and the woman who had been killed in the explosion.

Their deaths weren't fair. She remembered her grief, her anguish and the difficult years of therapy she'd undergone, never knowing if she'd regain her physical strength.

Kenneth Warrick deserved to suffer. But that wasn't her decision to make.

Reluctantly, she holstered her weapon.

Chapter Fourteen

Through the earbud, she heard Noah's voice. "Need some help?"

She gave him an indirect answer while staring at Warrick. "There was a time, Kenneth Warrick, when I would have been afraid to meet you alone. But not anymore—you don't scare me."

"Is that a good thing?"

"I'm a little bit surprised to see you. After everything went down at the Haymarket mansion, I figured you'd be in a hurry to crawl back into your rat hole. You know, the place where you've been hiding since you made too many enemies in Afghanistan to stay there."

"What makes you think I have enemies?" He strutted to an outcropping of rocks at the edge of the pool and struck a pose. "I have a fine lifestyle, better than yours. I don't have to stay at my parents' house."

"But you live under an alias, and you work as a part-time security guard. Your personal info doesn't show an address, just a box number. Sleeping in your car?" Her verbal jabs were partly to provoke him into revealing something useful and partly because she hated this guy with an enduring rage. "What's your latest scam, Warrick?"

"No time for a chat." He hopped down the rock and strolled along the path beside the pool and headed toward the trees. "Come with me."

She slipped into her jacket. "If you're trying to get me alone in the forest, forget it."

He halted, pivoted and faced her. Though she despised him, she had to admit that Warrick was good-looking in a rough, untamed way. A few inches above average height, he was long-legged and lean—the type of guy who looked good on a Harley. His dyed-blond hair, which was growing out at the roots, hung loose to his shoulders, and his scruffy facial hair was on the verge of becoming a beard. The small scar on his left eyebrow drew attention to his intense blue eyes, which had always been his best feature.

He squinted at her. "You want the truth, Gennie?"

"That'd be a nice change."

He stretched his long arm and pointed into the forest. "I want you to walk with me in that direction because I have a dirt bike stashed on that hill. When I'm done talking to you, I'm going to ride away from here and never come back to Colorado."

"Unless you're on trial for murder," she said.

"I didn't kill the little weasel."

"A dirt bike," she muttered. "You really enjoy making a dramatic getaway. I'm guessing that you were the person who escaped from the library on horseback."

"Cool, huh?"

A curse from Noah came through her earbud.

Clearly, he wasn't impressed with Warrick's idea of cleverness. "Why?" she asked.

"A diversion," he said, "and it worked. You and Noah chased after me, and the murderer slipped away in the darkness, easy-peasy."

"You're not the killer?"

"Hell, no."

"Who's your partner?" she demanded.

"As if I'm going to tell you."

"If you don't, the feds will blame you. You'll be arrested. You'll take the fall."

"No way. I'll be long gone. I owed the killer a debt. Now, we're square and I don't plan on any more reunions. I've got my own life to live, and I hear Costa Rica is nice in the springtime." He looked her up and down, his gaze lingering on her breasts. "You've still got a tight little body, Gennie. Maybe we could get something going, again. You could pay me a visit."

"Sure thing, leave me your address."

"Sweetheart, I'm no fool. I can't trust you with my personal info. When I want to see you, I'll sweep you up and carry you away."

As they neared the edge of the forest, she kept her hand on the butt of her Beretta. If he made a threatening move, she wouldn't hesitate to shoot him. Or would she? "Is there something you want to tell me?"

"When we were together, I didn't treat you right."

Huge understatement! "Go on."

"I always felt bad about the way we broke up. When I found out that you'd be at the fund-raiser, I sent that message with the flowers. I tried to warn you about the danger."

She didn't understand. "Was I in danger?"

"Slocum was always the target, but I didn't want to take a chance that you'd get injured in the crossfire. You should have taken the warning and gone home."

When would he understand that she would never turn tail and run? He couldn't scare her with bouquets of poisonous flowers and veiled threats. And he definitely couldn't tell her when to stay and when to go. Had she actually shed tears when their relationship ended? What had she been thinking? "Can I ask you a personal question?"

"Shoot."

"Answer with the first word that pops into your head." She paused, wanting to remember Murano's words correctly. "What is the single most important factor in a relationship?"

"That's easy," he said, "money."

She wondered how Murano would analyze that response. Did Warrick's callous greed arise from the scumbag chakra? She was done playing around with this guy. She wanted to squeeze out the last bit of information and take him into custody. He had just admitted to her that he knew the identity of the murderer. He had to face interrogation from the FBI. "When you showed yourself in the ballroom, was that also a warning?"

"That wasn't about you. There was someone else at the party I needed to contact."

"Who was that?" she asked.

"No names, Gennie."

"Who are you working for?" she asked. "Murano signs your paychecks. Is he involved in the murder?"

"Those paychecks are a pittance, nothing to get excited about." He stepped off the path as they neared the forest. "I do have another warning. This isn't over. Your friend is in danger."

"Ruby?"

"The general's wife? I don't know anything about her."

But he'd known enough to seduce her and draw her into an illicit kiss. The casual way he dismissed her illustrated his total lack of empathy. Poor Ruby was worried to death that her marriage was in jeopardy, and Warrick acted like he barely knew her. "You're an ass."

"Don't you want to know about your friend?"

"Are you talking about Loretta Slocum?" Gennie wouldn't have been surprised to hear that the people who killed the blackmailer were ready to go after Loretta and grab the evidence.

"I wasn't thinking of Loretta," he said. "But she's in danger as long as she has those documents in her possession."

Ironically, the cell phone was in Gennie's shoulder bag. "If you've got something to say, spit it out."

"Your boyfriend, Noah Sheridan, is in trouble."

Through the earbud, she heard Noah saying goodbye to Murano. To her, he said, "Don't let him leave."

Gennie stalled. "You don't know what you're talking about. Noah is my boss, not my boyfriend. There's nothing between us."

"Yeah, you keep telling yourself that." Still facing her, he walked backward up the hill. "I've been watching the two of you ever since you got to the Institute, and he looks at you like an alcoholic drools over a bottle of whiskey. And you're just as bad—all googly-eyed and twitchy."

"Twitchy?"

"You're wiggling your ass, pushing out your boobs."

"And you're disgusting." She didn't want him to get any farther away from her. The forest was thick with lots of boulders where he could hide. "Would you please stand still? Tell me why you think Noah is in trouble?"

"It wasn't a coincidence that he came into the murder room and nearly got arrested. Somebody is out to get him." He pursed his lips and blew her a kiss. "Have a nice life, sweetheart. I gave you something to work with, something you wanted. That's the last thing you're going to get from me."

"I don't forgive you."

"And I don't give a damn."

"You were involved in the explosion that killed my friends and nearly disabled me."

"I knew the warlord, and I'd spoken to him. But nobody was supposed to get hurt. You can believe me or not." He took another step away from her.

"Where do you think you're going?"

"Ask your boyfriend."

He pointed. She looked over her shoulder and saw Noah sprinting toward them on the path behind the lodge. He was over a hundred yards away. Through the earbud, she heard him breathing hard and telling her to stop Warrick.

When she whipped around, she yanked her Beretta from the holster, but she wasn't fast enough. He had the drop on her with Glocks in both hands. "Don't move,

Gennie." As he spoke, he continued to walk backward toward the forest.

"You don't want to shoot me," she said.

"That's right, I don't. You know that about me. I never want to hurt anybody, not here or in Afghanistan, and I sure as hell didn't kill Slocum."

"But you know who did." She took a step toward him. In her ear, she heard Noah panting for breath. He had to be close. "Come with me and talk to the police."

"Not today, sweetheart."

He dove to his right and ducked behind a boulder. She raised her arm and got off two shots before he returned fire. His bullet kicked up the dirt near her feet. Maybe he didn't want to kill her, but he didn't seem to have a problem inflicting another wound.

Standing in the open between the hot spring pool and the forest, she didn't have much in the way of natural cover. Crouching behind a shrub, she fired again. A branch near her shoulder was broken by Warrick's bullet.

Noah crashed onto the ground and pulled her down beside him. He struggled to catch his breath. "I heard what he said. He's got a bike hidden up there."

"We've got to stop him before he gets away."

"Cover me. I'm going after him."

Approaching a desperate man who was armed with two lethal handguns was a really bad idea, but she couldn't think of an alternative. To stop Warrick, they had to take a risk. She braced herself. When Noah took off running toward the hill, she emptied her gun, firing in the direction she'd last seen Warrick.

Noah found cover behind a tree and fired a couple of

shots. She took the moment to reload and peered up the hill toward the rock where he'd been hiding. Adrenaline flowed through her system, and her heart was pumping hard as she looked for Warrick.

He didn't seem to be returning fire. Had she scored a hit? What if she'd shot him? What if he was dead and she had killed him? In angry fantasies, she'd imagined this triumphant moment of revenge when she'd pay him back for all the pain and humiliation. But she felt no satisfaction, no joy. She was empty.

Noah motioned for her to move forward. In a crouch, she ran across the open space while Noah fired his gun. She joined him.

"I don't see him," Noah said.

"He might be injured." There was an unexplainable catch in her voice. "Or he might be dead."

"We'll proceed with caution. Maintain cover. I'll go right. You go left."

From her military training, she was familiar with this sort of exercise. She shoved the angst from her mind and concentrated on using the boulders and trees for cover as she climbed the hillside. *What if I killed him?* She couldn't think about that now.

Glancing across the forest, she saw Noah. He was wearing his sports jacket again—not the appropriate outfit for a chase through the forest, but he looked strong and tough. She was glad to have him for a partner and hoped he'd feel the same about her. She'd made a lot of mistakes today. Behind her back, she heard other people from the lodge approaching. She'd expected Murano's security team to respond to this disturbance.

And then, she recognized the unmistakable roar of a motorcycle starting up. Warrick was getting away.

Noah bolted upright and ran toward the sound. She followed.

They found a cluttered stack of branches that were probably used to hide the bike and tire tracks in the dirt. That was their only evidence. In the rustle of the wind through the boughs, she imagined she could hear Warrick laughing at her.

She lowered her Beretta. "I should have killed him when I had the chance."

INSTEAD OF RETURNING to his condo, Noah took her to his mountain home, the place where she'd picked the lock and kicked his ass. Though it was after nine o'clock and raining, he didn't mind spending the extra forty minutes on the road. At the cabin, he'd find the space, distance and uninterrupted time he needed to figure out what was happening. Warrick had said he was in trouble. Noah didn't know how and didn't know why, but he believed that lying bastard was telling the truth for once. Warrick didn't know him and didn't have a reason to lie. Noah accepted the strong possibility that somebody was out to get him.

As soon as he stepped across the threshold, turned on the light and glanced around his comfortable living room, a sense of calm and confidence descended over him. This property had been in his family for as long as he could remember. The logs were imbued with the indomitable Sheridan spirit. He and his brothers had collected the stones for the fireplace. After his brothers' deaths, Noah had come up here every weekend and every spare moment. His hard work on renovations and additions helped him manage his grief.

Gennie trooped through the door behind him, dropped the small suitcase she'd taken from her house yesterday and went straight to the kitchen. She'd been here twice before and knew where everything was. "I'll help myself," she said.

"I expected you would."

She grabbed a beer from the fridge, screwed off the top and took a long pull. During the hours they'd spent in the car, she'd been mostly silent, but that didn't mean she was passive. It had been a stressful day. Emotion seethed within her.

"I'm glad we came here," she said. "Murano might think his Institute is a beacon of serenity, but it doesn't hold a candle to this place. I can feel the happy memories."

"Plus there's a well-equipped gym upstairs."

"I could use a workout."

He got a beer for himself and opened the freezer unit, which was as big as the fridge and stocked with meat and frozen stuff that could be heated and served. They hadn't stopped for food on the way up here, and he was hungry. "Steak or veggie lasagna?"

"Is the lasagna homemade?"

"Not by me," he readily admitted. "I buy a lot of pre-made, frozen stuff from the diner down the road because I'm too lazy to cook. It's usually tasty."

"Let's try it."

She meandered over to the kitchen table and sat while he messed around with the oven and followed the directions that came with the pasta dish. They'd accomplished a great deal after they left Murano with profuse apologies for firing their weapons in a place dedicated to meditation and enlightenment. Never mind that the guru had been harboring a fugitive. Never mind that his security team was armed to the teeth. Guys like Murano could get away with bending the law.

As soon as Noah and Gennie were back in his SUV, he put through a call to the FBI agent in charge of the Slocum murder, informed him of what Warrick had said and told him where the FBI should start looking for a scumbag on a dirt bike. He also arranged to stop by the Haymarket mansion and drop off Loretta's phone.

Their return to the mansion had been uncomfortable on several levels. First of all, Noah was accustomed to being in charge and Tony Vega had taken over the senior position. Secondly, the positive relationship Noah had built with the general had crumbled when it became more apparent that Warrick wasn't smuggling arms and Slocum's death was related to a sleazy blackmail scheme that might tarnish reputations. Third, there were questions from the FBI.

The pen-twirling special agent who had irritated Gennie before didn't waste any time before lighting into her. He scolded about stealing crucial evidence and hampering their investigation. Noah shut him down... happily. He reminded the FBI team that Gennie had a Purple Heart, had served two and a half tours of duty and had trained at Quantico. Instead of getting on her case, they should thank her for seizing the phone from Loretta and squeezing out more information from Warrick. They'd be better served doing their jobs and tracking him down than griping at her. He hadn't made any friends with that little speech.

With the lasagna in the oven, he went to the kitchen table. Gennie had already contacted Anna Rose on the phone, and the sweet-faced grandma with her blue-streaked hair and polka-dot glasses stared at him from the screen.

"You two are going to be busy tonight," she said. "I sent a file with the data on Loretta's phone to your computer. Print it and read it. Start with Ruby's letter to the man she kissed."

"Why?" he asked.

"I have reason to believe she lied."

He went to the fridge and got another beer. This was going to be a very long night.

Chapter Fifteen

"Before we get started on the files," Gennie said, "there's something I need to talk about."

Noah sat across from her at the kitchen table, hoping he wouldn't hear about more trouble. "I'm listening."

"I've made some bad decisions today." She picked at the label on her beer bottle with her thumbnail. "It was my fault that Warrick got away. When he first walked up to me, he hadn't drawn his weapons. I could have winged him right then."

"You know as well as I do that an injured adversary is more dangerous."

"Don't make excuses for me, Noah. I had the opportunity to bring him down, but something stopped me. Shooting him didn't seem right."

In most cases, he believed that holding fire was usually prudent. "Why didn't it seem right?"

"Even though I hate the guy, I don't believe he killed Slocum."

"I agree."

"Still, I shouldn't have let him get away."

He agreed with that, too. But he understood her hesitation. In a similar circumstance, he might have done the same thing, and the end result of her conversation with Warrick was helpful. She got him to verify that there were two people in the library when Noah entered: Warrick and the killer. And Warrick admitted that he was the getaway man on horseback who lured them away from the house and allowed the real killer to escape. "You did a good job getting information from him."

"Shocking when you consider that interrogation isn't my strong point."

He sipped his beer to keep from laughing out loud. Gennie gave new meaning to blunt. She questioned people with all the subtlety of a bulldozer. "You charge right in, taking no prisoners."

"Psychology isn't my strong suit," she said. "I'd make a lousy profiler."

"There's a time for shrinks, and a time for soldiers." He looked through the window at the sheets of rain pouring down on the cedar deck. The warmth from the oven made the kitchen cozy and pleasant.

"Another mistake was stealing Loretta's phone and not telling the FBI about it right away."

"No harm done," he said. "We got the information to them, and we've got a copy. If they'd gotten their hands on it first, they never would have shared. Kudos on that mistake."

She stood and rolled her shoulders. "By far, the most wrong-minded thing I did all day was to go along with Ruby and Loretta when they hopped into her SUV and took off for Slocum's house."

He didn't want to undermine her confidence, but he couldn't tell her that she'd been wise. Gennie had been guarding those two women and should have been responsible for them. Instead, she let them call the shots and allowed them to charge headlong into a potentially dangerous situation.

She paced around his kitchen, energy shooting from her in bursts. "I'm lucky we didn't interrupt the person who tossed the house, lucky I didn't get both of them murdered. And I let Loretta steal Ruby's car. Have they located her?"

"Not yet."

She walked faster, back and forth, back and forth, spinning her wheels. "I tried to talk them out of it, but they were determined. Loretta in her silver platform heels and Ruby dressed like an episode from *I Love Lucy*, they wouldn't listen to me. They are the ones I should have shot—nothing serious, just a flesh wound."

"Stop." He stepped in her path and halted her by grasping her shoulders. "Don't blame yourself."

She leaned forward and collapsed against his chest. Her forehead rested on his collarbone as she inhaled and exhaled in ragged breaths. "I'm not crying."

"I didn't think you were."

"This sort of rash behavior isn't like me. I was trained to take orders and complete a mission. It seems like when I'm left to make decisions for myself, I mess up."

His instinct was to hold her, but he forced himself to exercise restraint. His feelings for Gennie were complicated, and he didn't want to give her the wrong idea. Clumsily, he patted her on the back. "You're new at this. You'll learn."

She slipped her hands inside his jacket and pulled him closer. Her breasts rubbed against his chest. He couldn't resist her, didn't want to hold himself apart. His arms encircled her. With a mutual sigh, they melted into the most satisfying embrace he'd ever experienced. He closed his eyes and inhaled the scent of her hair, still damp from their dash through the rain to his front door.

"I know something about decision-making," she said. "I had training in the military where it was my responsibility to lead four to twelve other soldiers and negotiate with villagers…and run from warlords."

He gave a murmur to show he was listening, but he didn't want a conversation, especially not about her military background. Why couldn't they lighten up and talk about flowers?

She snuggled against him. "In Afghanistan, I had time to figure things out and people I could talk to before I made a decision. My objectives were clear. It was our job to build things."

"Your work wasn't simple," he whispered into her ear. "You were on the other side of the world. The culture was different. There was a strong element of risk."

"I was never in combat," she said. "I never shot another human being."

She tilted her head to look up at him, and her eyes sparkled. Her lips were as delicate as rose petals. How could she be so angelic and tough at the same time? He stroked a strand of hair off her cheek. "No more talk of war."

"If I'd been on the front lines, if I had that experience, I might not have hesitated to shoot Warrick."

"Or the opposite," he said. "You might have decided to never touch a gun again."

"Have you ever shot anyone?" she asked.

"Twice, they both survived." And he refused to think about death and violence while he was holding a warm, beautiful woman in his arms. "Relax, Gennie. Listen to the rain. Smell the lasagna in the oven. There's nothing you can do to change what happened today. Just let it go."

"And how do I do that? How can I turn off my brain?"

"Breathe," he said.

After one short inhale and exhale, she gave a snort. "If this is something you learned from the MIME brochure, I wouldn't sign up for any lectures."

"For someone who's spent her whole life denying her feelings and claiming that nothing hurts, you've got a lot to say."

"I hadn't thought about it like that," she said. "What's wrong with me? Am I different from other people?"

"Maybe or maybe not." He stroked down her back to her slender waist. "Either way, I'm on your side. I'll stand by you."

As she continued to gaze up at him, her expression went from confrontational to agreeable to something else. The tension around her mouth relaxed, not that she was smiling but not snarling. The fire in her eyes turned into seductive warmth. Her eyelids lowered to half closed. She looked completely kissable. And so he did.

After a gentle taste of her lips, he separated from her. Searching her face, he looked for a signal. Had he stepped over a line? Turning back would be hell. His pulse had accelerated into high gear. He heard his heart banging like a snare. Blood rushed to his groin. He wanted more from her, needed more. "Gennie?"

"Yes," she said. "Yes, yes, yes."

There was nothing tentative about his second kiss. His tongue penetrated her mouth, and she engaged with him, kissing him back. Her passion nearly matched his.

She tightened her embrace. When he touched her breast, she gave an excited moan. He kissed her harder. Her legs tangled with his, putting pressure on his erection. She pushed so hard that he found himself pinned against the kitchen counter. And then, abruptly, she broke away from him.

Breathing hard, she stood a foot apart and clutched her hands against her breasts. "It's hot in here," she said. *You bet it is.* "Take off your jacket."

She peeled off the olive green top. Her sleeveless cream blouse had come completely untucked and hung loosely over her fitted olive trousers. In spite of the holster attached to her belt, she was incredibly sexy. She exhaled a long sigh. "I'm burning up."

He took off his own sports coat and tossed it over the back of a chair. "Another beer?"

She fluttered her hand near her face like a fan. "I need air."

She charged at the sliding glass door that led to the patio, and he had to move quickly to deactivate the alarm system and unfasten the lock. She glided the door open. Rain battered the deck, the roof and the surrounding trees.

The weather didn't deter her. She stepped out into the storm, opened her arms wide and turned her face upward, allowing the water to sluice through her hair and down her body. Slowly, she turned one hundred and eighty degrees. "Hooah," she shouted the US Army battle cry. She spun more quickly and shouted louder, "Hooah! Hooah!"

Laughing, she scampered back into the house. "Well, that was crazy."

Noah wouldn't dispute that call. "I'll get you a towel."

As he went down the hall to the linen closet beside the bathroom, he tried to figure out what had just happened. Expressing her confusion, frustration and self-doubt had somehow led to the kiss, which he liked very much. Then she dashed outside in the rain, screamed a battle cry and ended the whole thing with semi-hysterical laughter. Not his favorite moment with her.

Returning to the kitchen, he saw that she'd taken off her holster, placed the Beretta on the counter and was bent down to check the oven. He handed her two towels.

"I think the lasagna is done," she said as she rubbed the wetness from her hair. Did she really think they weren't going to talk about what had happened?

"I'll take care of the food. You sit at the table, unless you want to change clothes."

"I'm fine." She dried her bare arms and placed one of the towels on the chair before she sat. The other towel, she draped around her shoulders like a shawl. "I love a spring rain, don't you?"

The weather lashing his cabin windows wasn't a charming spring shower. This was the type of killer storm that caused mudslides and flash floods. "You're not cold?"

She thought for a moment and then shook her head. "I feel refreshed."

What the hell? He filled their water glasses, served the reheated lasagna and sat at the table beside her.

Surely there was a psychologically correct way to talk to her about what appeared to be the onset of a nervous breakdown, but he opted for her preferred interrogation method: blunt.

"You had an emotional explosion," he said, "a big one."

"Uh-huh." She shoved a big bite of pasta into her mouth.

"Has anything like that ever happened to you before?"

"Nope."

"What the hell, Gennie?"

She washed down her lasagna with a gulp of water. "I've seen a lot of therapists, and they'd probably diagnose post-traumatic stress, but I think you said it better."

"Me?"

"You told me that I tend to deny my emotions. I keep things buttoned down and refuse to feel pain. But I was so frustrated by the mistakes I made today that I couldn't hold it inside. If I didn't let off some steam, I'd explode. You said I should let it go."

"I did." When he'd cheerfully given that tidbit of advice, he'd been thinking of a heavy sigh or maybe a workout in the exercise room.

"Standing out there in the rain, I felt victorious. I don't know what prize I won, but I was glad."

He wasn't sure whether he should cheer or make reservations at the nearest psych ward. He opted for the former. "Congrats."

"I'm sorry about the kiss." She shrugged. "Your mouth just happened to be there."

"Back up, Gennie." He was willing to accept her

oversimplified explanation of the rain dance, but he refused to let that kiss be dismissed. She didn't accidentally plant her lips on his. "The kiss meant something. I was there. I felt it, too. You wanted me to kiss you."

"I did." She stared down at her plate of rapidly disappearing lasagna. "But I don't want the kiss to get in the way of our work or our friendship."

Though her logic didn't make sense, he agreed on one level. He didn't want to jeopardize what they had. He could force himself to be patient. "I understand."

"It's not like we could have a relationship," she said, "not according to Murano's test."

"The single question he asked?"

"That's right, lover boy."

He wasn't ashamed of his response. All things considered, he'd always choose love. "I could argue that Murano isn't the renowned authority he thinks he is. And I could point out that love and trust go together like peanut butter and jelly, but I'm not going to push."

She gave a nod. "I'm anxious to take a look at the data Anna Rose sent."

They changed gears, shifting to talk about the murder. His greatest concern had to be the trouble that Warrick predicted for him personally. Gennie's former fiancé was a scumbag, liar and accomplice to murder, but he'd made a good point. Noah had been summoned to the library. Someone—probably Warrick himself— had been ready and waiting with a stun gun and drugs. What was the purpose? It seemed likely that they were trying to frame him. But why?

After they finished their dinner, he put on a pot of decaf coffee and they went into the large downstairs office/meeting room between the living room and kitchen. Originally, this cabin had been a hunting lodge with few amenities. Twelve years ago, when he'd started renovating after Josh's death, he hadn't been thinking of a training facility for ARC. But that was how it turned out. The first floor was dedicated to group activities, like meetings and eating. The upstairs was bedrooms with a smaller office and the workout room.

He set up a large screen computer on a long desk built into the wall. Gennie sat on a swivel chair with wheels and scooted up close to see the first image.

"Make it the letter from Ruby," she said. "I'm dying to see it."

"Here's a question," he said. "Why send a letter?"

"It's odd and old-fashioned. Maybe she wanted to mark the occasion."

He shrugged. "Or it could be a romantic gesture. The original might be on pastel paper, might be scented."

"Don't make me gag," she said. "We're talking about a letter to Kenneth Warrick."

At the same time he displayed the letter on the computer screen, he made two copies—one for her and one for him. Tonight, they'd be dealing with a lot of data, and having hard copies would allow them to check the evidence at their own speed.

He was content with rapidly scanning this page. "She talks about *their special night* and she'll never forget him, blah, blah."

"There's so much more," Gennie said. "First, Ruby's penmanship is lovely, almost as though she copied it from a cursive handbook."

He didn't see the significance. "So?"

"It shows that she took care with her writing. And she uses a bunch of pretty images, like saying that the wind in her hair was *gentle as butterfly wings* and *bathing in the sheer radiance of pure silver starlight.*"

"None of this proves anything except that she was hot for this dude." He handed Gennie a hard copy. "Why did Anna Rose think Ruby lied?"

"Here's your answer." Gennie pointed to the words on the screen and read, "Your beautiful eyes, darker than mocha latte are the rich color of chocolate."

"I don't get it."

"Chocolate eyes," she repeated. "He has chocolate eyes."

"And?"

"Slocum was platinum blond with watery blue eyes. Warrick's best feature has always been his blue, blue, blue eyes."

"Ruby was kissing someone else," he said. "She lied."

"And who is this mystery man." She stared at him. "Any ideas, brown eyes?"

Now he was being framed for a kiss. What next?

Chapter Sixteen

Under the pretext of scrutinizing his eyes, Gennie leaned close to Noah and stared. She should have been concentrating on solving this latest clue, but looking into his eyes was deeply distracting, almost intoxicating. "Your eyes are warmer, more like whiskey than chocolate."

"Am I off the hook?"

"Oh, please. I never really thought you were the guy who made out with the general's wife. You're a businessman. You'd never risk ARC's reputation for a kiss."

Still, he was a spectacularly good kisser. In the back of her mind, their embrace was replaying on an endless loop. When she remembered his kiss, her lips tingled, and her body temperature elevated to a feverish level. Afterward when they talked, she'd been glad that he called her bluff when she tried to dismiss their intimacy. That kiss meant something.

"What else does she say in the letter?" he asked.

"Why ask me? You can read it for yourself."

"But I probably wouldn't notice the right things. I'm a guy, I don't understand the code. That's why I didn't realize that eye color was a big deal."

"Code? I hope you aren't implying that there's a *girl code* when it comes to describing men. If you are, I'm insulted."

"Not an insult," he said emphatically. "Men and women perceive the world from different angles. That's just the way life is. You see things that I don't. The same goes for me."

Though she basically agreed with him, she sensed his discomfort with this topic. Noah was digging himself a hole, and she wanted to see how he'd get out of this. "What kind of things do we see differently?"

"An example," he said. "Your first impressions are likely based on clothes and style."

"And what do men notice?"

Without thinking, he cupped invisible breasts. His gesture disappeared in a flash as he leveled a palm at his chin. "Height, men notice height."

And hooters. She'd been in the army long enough to know that most of the guys could tell a woman's breast size but had no idea of her eye color. To be fair, she'd done her share of objectifying a good-looking guy with a nice firm bottom, like Noah's. She cleared her throat. "What else do you notice?"

"Tone of voice," he said. "Can't stand screeching or whispering."

"Same here."

"And hair, natural hair—like yours—is the best."

She fluffed her still damp tendrils. "I'll be sure to compliment the stylist who does my highlights."

"A woman would have known your hair was dyed." He looked away from her, squinting at Ruby's words on the computer screen. "We've gotten off on a tangent."

She teased, "Does this mean that you're not ready to hunker down and defend your position?"

"One thing I learned from my mostly forgotten former marriage is how to pick my fights. This position isn't worth defending. I'd drop it."

He balled his fingers into fists and then snapped them open—a dramatic gesture that somehow erased the impending argument. She appreciated the way he had avoided conflict by acknowledging their differences and then moving forward. Popping her fingers open, she mimicked his release. "Let's get back to work."

"Now that we know Ruby lied, we should figure out why. What's she trying to hide?"

Gennie read through the letter a couple more times. Basically, Ruby described a romantic tryst in the early evening. The location was in the mountains where there were forests and rough stones. She was up so high that she felt like she could touch the stars. The moment was special and she'd never forget him, but she loved her husband and never wanted to see Mr. Chocolate Eyes again. She signed it with *fondly*.

"Ruby mentions wind in her hair, so they were outside. In the mountains surrounded by trees and rugged stones, their location was up high." She concluded, "The description reminds me of the tower at MIME."

"Damn," Noah said. "It was Murano."

"His eyes are the right color."

"It makes a kind of perverse sense. When I saw Ruby before the fund-raiser, she made it clear that she couldn't stand Murano and didn't want him in her house."

"Like it says in her letter, she never wanted to see him again."

"Fist bump," Noah said as they tapped knuckles. "Good work."

Thinking like a detective was new to her, and she was enjoying the mental exercise. The idea of Ruby hooking up with Murano made way more sense than sharing a tryst with Warrick, a sexy bad boy who would have been a definite downgrade on the social scale. "I feel bad for the general. He's playing golf and throwing fund-raisers for the guy who was messing around with his wife."

"Maybe that's why she lied. She didn't want to embarrass Roger. I've got to say, I kind of respect her for that."

"When you were married, did your wife ever cheat?" As soon as the words came out, she regretted them. *Too blunt.* "Forget I said that."

"No problem. I consider my former marriage to be a cautionary tale. Infidelity wasn't a problem, not for her or for me. We never betrayed each other."

So, he was trustworthy. Gennie liked that. As long as she was being blatantly nosy, she might as well get the whole story. "Why did you break up?"

"We both had strong opinions and nothing in common. Did I mention that she's an attorney? Our arguments were epic."

Across the room on a long table, his cell phone jangled, and he went to pick it up. After a glance at the phone's screen, he put the call on Speaker and said, "Hey, Tony, what's up?"

"Sorry to call so late."

"It's only ten thirty, and I want you to keep me posted

on any developments, no matter what the time. Where are you?"

"I came back to the Haymarket house after I got a call from Zoey on the night shift. Loretta Slocum came back."

Gennie was relieved to hear that the feisty little woman from Nashville had ended her joy ride in the deluxe SUV without further mishap. "Did she say anything?"

"Is that Gennie?" Tony asked.

"I'm staying at the cabin with Noah until the security on my house is completed. He's got plenty of extra room."

"Are you getting a lot of rain up there?"

"A monsoon," Noah said. "Tell us about Loretta."

"According to Zoey, she apologized for stealing Ruby's car. She'd been searching but hadn't found the documents that she was sure Dean had hidden. Supposedly, her brother-in-law had three properties, and she'd checked out the south Denver house and the rental near Boulder. She couldn't locate the place in the mountains. She was weepy. Zoey felt sorry for her."

Gennie had zero sympathy. Though Loretta wasn't a blood relation to Dean, they shared a couple of traits. Both were driven by greed. Both were manipulators. "What else?"

"That's all," Tony said. "She's still here at the house. The FBI has her sequestered for interrogation."

"This time, they need to hang on to her," Noah said.

Gennie cringed inside. She was to blame for Loretta's first escape—a mistake she'd never make again. There was such a thing as being too trusting.

"What are you doing at the cabin?" Tony asked.

"Going through the documents that were on Loretta's phone. If we're lucky, we might find something that will lead us to the mountain property."

"I could help," Tony said.

"I'd rather have you stay in town and keep an eye on the mansion. In the morning, we'll be headed down there. We'll see you then." He ended the call and returned to the computer. On the long desk were two stacks of papers—his and hers copies of the information from Loretta's phone. He passed one of the stacks to her. "I've barely glanced at this stuff, but I think we can sort it into categories."

Rifling through the loose sheets, she saw a photograph of what might have been a naked man and woman clutching each other. She turned the photo horizontal and then vertical again. "It looks like this picture was taken through half-closed blinds. I can't exactly tell what I'm looking at, and the people are unrecognizable."

"It's hard to believe Slocum could get a blackmail payment using this photo."

In her mind, the whole arrangement was unbelievable. This man and woman were betraying their partners and compounding the original lie by engaging in a cover-up. Equally sleazy was Dean Slocum. There were four other photos, similar in the sense that faces weren't shown and random body parts squeezed against each other.

Noah set the photos aside, facedown on the desk. "I don't think we'll learn much by studying those pictures."

"And they're gross." She stood, stretched and yawned. "I suddenly feel the need for a shower."

"I'll come upstairs with you," he said. "I wouldn't mind changing out of these clothes."

She grabbed her little suitcase at the front door and followed Noah up to the second floor. She vividly remembered the layout from her first experience breaking into the cabin to "rescue the hostage." They walked past the office at the top of the stairs and went toward the gym at the end of the hall.

Noah opened the last door on the left across from the gym. "This is the master bedroom, my bedroom, the only one with an attached bathroom. You have your choice of the guest bedroom across the hall and the one next to mine."

She chose to sleep in the room beside his. In the morning, her room would have the same exposure to sunlight as his, and they'd wake at the same time. "I'll clean up and meet you downstairs."

Inside her cozy bedroom, she went directly to the queen bed with a knotty pine frame and collapsed onto the firm mattress. The rain splattering against the windowpanes made a soothing rhythm. It would have been easy to close her eyes and drift off to sleep, but she wanted to stay awake. Not only was she curious about the blackmail documents but she wanted to take advantage of this time alone with Noah.

Usually, there were a half dozen ARC employees hanging around, demanding bits of his time and asking questions. More than a boss, Noah Sheridan was their leader. Tony might be capable of doing the supervisory basics, but he'd never fill Noah's shoes.

While she rinsed herself in a steaming hot shower, Gennie considered the stack of ugly information Slocum had compiled on his acquaintances and associates. This evidence of his extortion plots provided ample motives for murder. Most likely, one of the people he was blackmailing had reached their limit. They snapped and killed him.

How could they possibly guess who?

She dressed in colorful layers, starting with yoga pants patterned like blue, red and pink ocean waves. Her T-shirt was purple and yellow. The lightweight cardigan she wore on top was turquoise. She replaced the wrap on her ankle and slipped on a pair of worn sneakers that felt like they'd been custom-made for her feet.

After she dragged a brush through her hair, she glanced in the bathroom mirror. Her lack of makeup was obvious. Though Gennie dyed her hair, she was a natural blond with blond eyelashes that were almost invisible. Should she take a moment to apply mascara and liner? If she did, he might think she was trying too hard. If not, she was too plain.

No time to worry about her appearance. She wasn't staying at the cabin to further her relationship with Noah. This was work! She turned away from her unadorned face in the mirror and tromped downstairs in unsexy sneakers and loose-fitting workout clothes. Bottom line: she wouldn't mind seducing her boss but wanted to pull it off without appearing to be seductive. Might be impossible; she really didn't have feminine wiles.

He'd beaten her downstairs. His short hair was spikey wet from a shower, and he'd dressed in jeans and a flannel shirt. He took a position in front of a whiteboard. Across the top, he'd written headers. "These are the basic reasons for blackmail. Scandal is the most obvious, usually involving sex and cheating."

"And that's where we file those creepy photos."

"You guessed it," he said. "Lies come next. These are mostly business lies or military lies that somebody told to get ahead or to throw an enemy under the bus."

She read the next header aloud. "Secrets? Give me an example."

"Things that happened in the past." He passed her an email. "This tells the sad story of how one sister tricked the other out of the family inheritance."

"Motives," she said. "These secrets are all motives for murder."

"I figured if we broke it down into three categories—Scandal, Lies and Secrets—we could put these documents into some kind of order."

Carrying her designated stack of data, she returned to her swivel chair and sat with her feet up on the long desk, reading through one sordid tale after another. In most of them, the names had been redacted, which explained why Loretta was desperate to find the originals. Apparently, Slocum didn't trust his sister-in-law to keep her hands off his business. "I'm guessing that the FBI will have more luck than we will in matching identities to the documents."

"Anna Rose is working that angle for us."

Though Gennie appreciated the skills and talents of Anna Rose Claymore, she didn't think the lady with polka-dot glasses was a match for the feds. "The FBI has more resources."

"Different resources," he said. "I don't understand how Anna Rose comes up with some of the data she finds. Could be something to do with the dark web or underground hackers. But she's amazing."

"If I notice anything suspicious, I'll flag it for her."

As the night dragged on, these stories of bad behavior began to meld into one large ugly vision of humanity. There were betrayals, partners attacking each other, hatreds and schemes. She read a suicide note and wondered if the person who wrote it was actually dead.

Every twenty minutes, she made a point of getting up and moving around. If she froze in one position for too long, the muscles that lacked sensitivity tended to seize up, especially in rainy weather. After the third reading of a document about foreclosure, she recognized a name on the page and bounded to her feet. Her left leg didn't hurt, but it wobbled precariously. She took a moment to stabilize before she announced, "Murano."

Noah stepped up beside her. "Are you okay?"

"It's just a glitch." She placed the document in his hand. "I'm guessing this is about the MIME property and it mentions Murano."

"Look again," he said.

She read, reread and groaned. The name she'd been so thrilled to find was Marciano. "I could have sworn it was Murano. Everything else fits. The description of the location, including the original lodge, sounds like his Institute."

"It's dated fifteen years ago," he said. "MIME started after that."

"Marciano could be a fake name. Remember when he told us that he wasn't part of the actual family back in Italy? Maybe he changed his name before he started his import business."

"One of his political opponents would have dug up evidence of an alias, but I'll ask Anna Rose to check his history." Noah stayed at her side, watching her with a concerned expression. "We should take a break."

"I'm fine. This just feels like when your foot goes to sleep." Walking slowly to keep from betraying her momentary weakness with a limp, she went to the kitchen and got a water bottle from the fridge. Staying hydrated solved a lot of physical problems.

Noah stood in the doorway behind her. "I wish that document had turned out to be a real link to Murano. He's sneaky and shady. Plus, being a politician makes him an excellent target for blackmail."

"In your documents, have you found anything interesting?"

"There's some military correspondence, dated from the time that my brother was killed. I don't know how that could turn into blackmail, but I've been trying to remember the names of the other guys who died in the same action with Josh." He winced at the painful memory. "There's nothing in those emails that I didn't know before."

"We still haven't found a threat to you."

"Warrick might have made it up."

She glanced at the wall clock in the kitchen. "It's after midnight. How much longer are we going to do this?"

"It's okay with me if you go to bed."

With you? That was a blunt question that she kept to herself. "I'll stay up. Maybe the next time I see Murano's name, it'll make sense."

As she followed him back to the meeting room, she

noticed how good he looked in his snug-fitting jeans. Earlier tonight, they'd been on track to spending the night in the same bed. Somehow, their intimacy had gone off the rails. Though she tried to tell herself that moving forward slowly was the best course, Gennie was disappointed.

Grumpily, she slouched in her swivel chair and went back to work. She kept coming back to two official-looking birth certificates. One was twenty-eight years old, from the state of Colorado. The other had been issued two years ago at a hospital in Albuquerque. The mother's names were listed and the children's. But the spaces for "father" were blank.

She waved the papers at him. "What secrets could these be hiding?"

"One is for a grown man. The other is for a baby. I don't see anything significant about the names, but I mentioned the certificates to Anna Rose. She'll research the history of these people. I expect the FBI will do the same."

"How would a blackmailer use these?"

Noah wrote *birth certificates* on the whiteboard under *Secrets* as he talked. "Maybe the father didn't know he had a child until the kid showed up on the doorstep and demanded his inheritance."

"That is so sad. I'd rather think that the illegitimate son approached him and they had a wonderful reunion."

"Dean Slocum didn't get rich from happy endings."

When she went back to the research, Gennie came to a realization. "This is what detective work is really like, isn't it? It's all about gathering evidence, poking through documents and seeing the worst in people."

"I was a beat cop, never a detective, but you're right. Most crime is straightforward and obvious. There's no question about who did it."

"Like when the killer is standing over the body with a smoking gun," she said.

"There's not usually so much drama, but yeah. In a case like Slocum's murder, the killer and his accomplices went to a lot of trouble to muddy the waters. Figuring it out requires patience and perseverance."

"Not my best skills."

When Gennie knew what she wanted, she went after it. She looked across the room at Noah. Their gazes met. Without speaking, they communicated, and she got the message, which wasn't what she'd hoped for. *Nothing intimate. No more kisses. Not tonight.*

The Final Seduction

Chapter Seventeen

The next morning, Noah rolled out of bed, brushed his teeth, drank a glass of water and hit the gym. Four and a half hours of sleep wasn't enough. He was still tense and in need of physical release. After stretching to loosen up, he set the treadmill at an easy jogging pace. He would have gone running outdoors if it hadn't rained so much yesterday. It was too muddy.

He gradually ramped up the treadmill speed. The investigation should have been first and foremost in his mind, especially since they still hadn't uncovered the reason for Warrick's warning. But Noah's mind filled with images of Gennie. He remembered how curvy she looked in that black jumpsuit she wore at the fundraiser, how fierce when she faced Warrick holding her Beretta two-handed and how crazy when she spun around in the rain on his deck. Most of all, he thought about last night when they were working side by side. She hadn't noticed him watching her. Completely unselfconscious, she twirled a piece of hair between her slender fingers. As she read the documents, an array of emotions played across her face—ranging from disgust at the material to excitement when she thought she'd discovered something important.

Fascinating and sexy, she drew him toward her like a magnetic force. Last night, he had to set aside the documents because all he could think about was sweeping her off her feet and carrying her to his bed. What stopped him? For sure, there were valid reasons. He barely knew her. Sleeping with an employee was irresponsible. His attraction to strong women had gotten him into trouble before. He had to be patient. Later, there would be time for them.

Behind his back, he heard the door to the gym open. Gennie called out, "I'm impressed. It's not even six o'clock, and you're already working out."

"And I'm not a morning person." He waited for her to saunter into view. "Are you?"

"Not really." She draped herself across the front of the exercise machine and gave him a crooked smile. "Want coffee?"

I want you. He had the feeling that she could provide a wake-up call he'd never forget. "Coffee's good."

Her striped flannel nightshirt fell almost to her knees, exposing the lower half of her smooth sexy legs. He noticed light scarring from her injuries and operations. Those marks showed her character and enhanced her beauty.

Casually, she reached over and adjusted the speed on the treadmill so he was forced to run faster. "What's our plan for today?"

"I'm waiting to hear back from Anna Rose." Struggling to maintain the new pace, he was breathing harder. "Maybe go to the general's."

"Do you have something specific you're expecting Anna Rose to find?"

"Yeah."

"What is it?"

"Baer," he said,

"Are you talking about a teddy bear? A grizzly bear?"

"Robert Baer."

She adjusted the speed higher. He was sprinting, dammit, sprinting.

Last night, he'd finally remembered the name of his brother's friend who had also been killed in combat. Noah had actually met Robert Baer who was tight with Josh.

Gennie hit the stop button. "I need an explanation."

As soon as the treadmill slowed, he jumped off. Doubled over, he was breathing hard, sweating. "Don't ever do that again."

"Which part? The speed run or the quick stop?" Her evil little grin told him that she wasn't the least bit sorry that he was winded.

"Neither," he said as he straightened his spine.

She perched on the weight bench. "Tell me about this Robert Baer."

"I remembered his name last night, sent it to Anna Rose." He stretched his shoulders and flexed. "Baer was one of Josh's best buddies. They were both Rangers."

"And you think Baer might be the reason Slocum saved that stuff about the mission that killed your brother," she said.

"It's worth looking into," he said. "Baer came home with Josh on leave a couple of times. I don't think he had any family, but he always had money to throw around when we went snowboarding,"

"How old were you?"

"Seventeen or eighteen, it was a couple of years before my brother died. Baer loved this cabin, which was nowhere near as cool as it is now. He kept saying that he wanted to live in Colorado."

A sad irony brushed over him. Robert Baer had gotten his wish. He was here in Denver, buried at Fort Logan Cemetery in a grave beside Josh. They were together for eternity.

Gennie left her perch, came up beside him and placed her hand on his arm. He didn't need to explain his sadness to her. She knew.

"I'll get that coffee started," she said.

He followed her from the gym and paused at the door to his bedroom. "I've got to grab my cell phone. See you downstairs."

When he picked up his phone on the bedside table, he was surprised to see a new text message from Anna Rose, telling him to check his computer. Didn't that woman ever sleep? He'd sent Baer's name after midnight. When did she have time to research?

In the bathroom, he splashed water on his face and pits and toweled off. He threw on a sweatshirt before he went downstairs to the kitchen where the aroma of coffee swirled in the air. Few things in the world smelled as good as coffee brewing in the morning.

Gennie glanced in his direction. "I found something labeled Cinnamon Rolls in the freezer. I'm popping it into the oven."

He filled his mug. "Grab your coffee and come with me. Anna Rose sent us something on the computer."

"Is this about Baer? Why couldn't she just tell you about it on the phone?"

"Phone lines aren't secure," he said. "No communication is truly safe anymore, but Anna Rose installed major encryption software on her computer and a couple of others in ARC. Apparently, she doesn't want anybody else to hack in. The information she's sending must be important."

"Or dangerous," Gennie said under her breath.

In the meeting room, he went to the long wall desk and turned on his computer. On the main screen, he saw a new icon that had to be from Anna Rose. He clicked. It opened. And there she was, Anna Rose Claymore in person. Her pajamas were printed with flamingoes, and the frames for her glasses were emerald green.

"Good morning, kids." She toasted the screen with a mug that said *World's Greatest Granny.* "We're talking live on a dedicated feed, and you should ask me everything you need to know right now. We might be out of touch for a while."

"Why?" Gennie asked. "Are we going somewhere?"

"Yes, and you need to use extreme caution."

"Where?"

"Let me start at the beginning, dear." She cleared her throat, preparing to lecture. "Certain aspects of this murder required inside access. Someone had to unlock the library window so Warrick could get inside. This person might not be the murderer but is certainly an accomplice. This could be an inside job. Therefore, you should trust no one."

Noah agreed. Though it was difficult to suspect Henry Harrison or any of the other staff who worked at the mansion, logic pointed to an insider. "I hate to say this. What about the ARC employees?"

"Sadly, you should consider them as suspects."

"What did you learn about Baer?"

"Digging up information on this young man wasn't easy. A lesser genius wouldn't have found a thing. Not to toot my own horn, but my computer work on this subject is certifiably brilliant."

"All hail, Anna Rose." He sipped his coffee.

"Robert Baer," she said, "was orphaned in his early teens. His wealthy parents left him a ton of money, which was protected by an attorney who acted as Baer's guardian until he was twenty-one. They had a falling out. The young man severed all ties with his guardian and everyone else. He ran off and joined the army, which turned out to be a wise decision because he excelled in the military environment, rising through the ranks and becoming a Ranger. That's where he met Dean Slocum."

Noah set his coffee mug down on the desktop. On a subconscious level he'd known that Slocum and Baer knew each other. Still, the connection was ominous. "What else?"

"I don't want to upset you, dear."

"I'm okay." But he felt the ghosts of old dead suspicions whispering through him, chilling his blood and turning his heart to ice.

"Blackmail was only one of Slocum's talents. He had his sticky fingers in all kinds of nefarious schemes. With Baer, he pulled off a land grab."

Noah needed to know more. His patience was wearing thin. "Are you saying that he stole land from Baer?"

"Not directly. Slocum somehow convinced Baer to put his name on the deed of a property that's close to your cabin. Do you remember anything about the land?"

A vague recollection formed in the back of his memory. The three of them—Josh, Baer and him—drove to a couple of acres that Baer wanted to buy so he could build his own cabin and they could be neighbors. "I might have gone there."

"There are directions in this file," Anna Rose said. "I believe this is the property that Loretta has been searching for. Technically, Slocum owned it, but the records are all in Baer's name. The setup is legally shaky, but Baer died without a will and had no one looking out for his interests. Slocum took advantage of him. His plan must have been to get clear title and sell for a tidy profit."

Gennie said, "Do you think we should go to this property?"

"Loretta seemed to think there was something valuable there," Anna Rose replied. "It's worth taking a look around. You might find the original blackmail documents."

Noah's reading of the situation was different. "When Baer was killed, Slocum inherited."

"That's not entirely accurate."

"Why not? Slocum gained control of the mountain property. He benefited from Baer's death."

"Yes, dear. But there are other factors to—"

He interrupted her with a question that had haunted him ever since his brother was killed in action. Supposedly, the attack on his platoon was due to mistaken intelligence. "Did Slocum engineer Baer's death? Did he purposely direct Baer and Josh and their whole platoon into lethal danger?"

Anna Rose took off her glasses and rubbed the worry line between her eyebrows. "There's no way of knowing what was going on in Slocum's twisted mind, but I doubt he wanted Baer to come to injury. He was manipulating that unfortunate young man. There was at least one other property involved."

"The one with the foreclosure notice," Gennie said. "Was that MIME property?"

"I'll need to dig deeper, but I think you might be correct."

Gennie bounced to her feet. "You really are brilliant."

"Thank you, dear."

"I love the way you've connected the dots—from Baer to Slocum to Murano who might be using the alias Marciano. Brilliant!" She waved. "I need to run to the kitchen and check on my buns."

"Wait!" Anna Rose reached out as if she could grab Gennie. "Do you have any other questions?"

She looked up and to the right, typical of someone who was searching for a recent memory. "The birth certificates," she said. "Is there any more information on them?"

"Very little. I learned that the mother on the certificate from twenty-eight years ago passed away before her child was five. No new information on the fathers."

"What about Ruby and the letter?" Gennie asked. "Has she gotten up the nerve to tell the general?"

"Indeed, she has. He's already forgiven her." Anna Rose pinched her lips. "For kissing his supposed friend, Mitch Murano."

"I'm glad they're being honest with each other. Goodbye, Anna."

He watched as Gennie flitted from the room. She was a wonderful distraction, but he had other things on his mind. The possibility of Slocum causing Josh's death weighed heavily.

"Look at me," Anna Rose said.

"Yes, ma'am."

"Your personal relationship to Baer and Slocum is a problem. The FBI already suspects you, and the deeper connection makes it worse." She frowned and leaned closer to her computer screen, as if that would improve her vision. "I see that look in your eye, Noah. We don't have time to indulge in angst. Do you understand me?"

Ruefully, he nodded. He and Gennie lived at opposite ends of the spectrum when it came to pain. She didn't feel a thing while he tended to wallow in the sadness. "Don't worry. I won't go off the rails. My angst—as you call it—is motivation. I renovated this cabin while I mourned my brother. Gennie and I will solve this thing and restore ARC's stellar reputation."

"I'm sure you will. Right now, I want you to go to Baer's property and search. Though I'd like to hold this information close to the vest, I'm obligated to tell the FBI investigators."

"How long have we got?"

"I'll make that call in a few hours, around nine o'clock," she said. "Take extreme security precautions. Disable any device that might be used to track you. If you're getting close to a solution, the murderer will be threatened."

"I'll handle it."

"Be careful, dear. And take care of Gennie. Something is developing between you and this young woman." Anna Rose beamed. "I approve."

He was a grown man and didn't need anyone's blessing. Still, he appreciated her opinion. He and Gennie were good together.

Chapter Eighteen

Gennie believed the information collected by Anna Rose. More importantly, she believed the threat. She and Noah were in danger.

Before they left his house, she dressed for battle with her Beretta, her second gun in the ankle holster, a stun gun and a double-edged blade in a belt sheath. Maybe a bit of overkill, but she wanted to be prepared. Her hiking boots provided ankle support but were still lightweight. In the pockets of her cargo pants, she had various items, including extra ammo clips, zip ties to use as handcuffs, bungee cords, a lighter and granola bars in case her energy dipped low. If she'd been wearing her army camo jacket, she would have had even more pockets to fill. But she hadn't thought far enough ahead to bring it. Her jean jacket fit neatly over a thin custom-made bulletproof vest.

Riding in the passenger seat, she experienced a familiar surge of adrenaline. They were embarking on a mission that required her to be alert and observant, engaging all her training and skill. Before Noah started the car, he'd disconnected the internet and the GPS so they couldn't be tracked. He gave their cell phones a similar treatment. Out of touch with any other communication or unwanted surveillance, they were in stealth mode.

A few minutes before seven o'clock, they drove away in his SUV, which had been locked in the garage at his cabin. She wished she could say it was a beautiful morning, but rain clouds draped across the skies like a heavy curtain. The gray fog was thick enough that Noah had to use the headlights.

As he drove, she studied his profile. His brow furrowed as he stared straight ahead through the windshield. His jaw was tense, and he gripped the steering wheel with both hands. His intensity spoke more than words. From Anna Rose's report, Noah had learned that his brother's death might have been part of a larger scheme that Slocum was running. Though not a proven fact, the information was enough to send Noah into a downward spiral.

In the military, she'd learned more than she ever wanted to know about death and sorrow. There was no magical wand she could wave to take away his sadness. Her only option was to accept his pain and be there for him.

"If you want to talk," she said, "I'll listen."

"Not right now."

"That's cool."

His house was about six miles off the highway on a narrow road that wove through forest and canyon as it followed the path of a creek that was usually a trickle. Rainfall and spring runoff from melting snow had swelled the rushing water. In some places, it gushed over the banks. In spite of poor visibility, Noah raced along. He must have driven this route hundreds of times.

She wouldn't presume to tell him to watch where he was going, but she couldn't help noticing that his gaze was fixed intently on the rearview mirrors.

She turned in her seat and peered through the back window. Far behind them, she caught a glimpse of headlights. "Are we being followed?"

"I can't tell," he said. "It's almost seven, not too early for someone to be on the road for legitimate reasons."

"You're driving extra fast," she said. "Are the headlights keeping up?"

"Yes."

"How far is it to Baer's property?"

"According to the directions from Anna Rose, we'll be there in less than half an hour. I have no idea what we'll find."

"Didn't you go there with your brother and Baer?"

"That was a lifetime ago. I was a dorky teenager, totally impressed by these two manly men. I hardly noticed where we were, but I'm sure there wasn't a cabin on the property. Baer had to hold off on new construction until paperwork cleared. There was a problem with water rights and Baer wanted to drill a well, even though the property is near a good-sized creek."

As a Colorado native, she knew that building in the mountains could require tons of permits and appearances at water board meetings, which was a difficult prospect when the owner was in the army, stationed on the other side of the world. "So there might not even be a house?"

"Or the whole area could be a thriving development. Who knows what could have happened in thirteen or fourteen years."

At the stop sign on the intersection with the main road, he halted and waited for the vehicle that had been behind them to appear. Two minutes passed, and there was nothing.

"I saw the headlights," she said. The other vehicle had either turned off before reaching the main road or remained in the shadows, lurking. "I know he was there."

"I'm hoping he doesn't have a way to trace us." His dire expression lightened with a grin. "This is like the good old days when drones and satellite surveillance couldn't watch every move we make."

She guessed at his plan. "You're going to drive like a maniac and lose the tail."

"Hang on."

He whipped a left onto the highway, headed away from Baer's property. The road was damp but not icy. In April, it was usually too warm for snow. Hail was more likely, but Noah wasn't thinking about the weather. They were flying, swooping around the curves and accelerating on the straightaway.

Gennie loved to go fast, whether in a car or motorcycle or boat. Her favorite sport was downhill skiing with the wind in her hair. For her, speed was a full-body experience that elevated her to a different level, almost like sex. And she could tell that Noah felt the same way. When she glanced over at him, his fire and excitement were obvious.

Centrifugal force threw her against the passenger door when he made a sharp left onto another two-lane road. Before she could catch her breath, they rocketed up a steep ascent, took another left and another right onto a gravel road, which immediately forked. Noah steered the SUV to the right. His skill at mountain driving was the only reason they hadn't skidded off the road and plummeted down a steep cliff.

He killed his headlights, turned into a driveway and parked. "Let's see if he kept up."

She gave a little whoop. "Can we do that again?"

In a few quick moves, he unfastened his seat belt, drew his weapon and slipped out of the car. "Are you coming?"

"You bet."

With her Beretta clenched in her fist, she joined him at the right of the SUV where they hid in the shadows of tall pine trees and waited. There were no lights from the house behind the driveway and no other vehicles on the road, but the forest wasn't silent. Raindrops splattered on the leaves and branches. The wind rustled.

She tugged the brim of her baseball cap, pulling it lower on her forehead. How long should they wait? If the vehicle that had been following them appeared, what should they do? An exchange of gunfire seemed like a really bad idea, especially since she and Noah didn't know who was in pursuit.

He shrugged. "I think we lost them."

"Not surprised. Where did you learn to drive like that?"

"I'd like to say that I trained in evasive driving techniques, but I learned the old-fashioned way—being a teenager who liked to go fast and take risks. Most of the time, I got it right."

"What happened when you got it wrong?"

His sheepish grin was a relief from the tension that

had been tying him in knots. "On one memorable occasion, I drove my mom's car halfway across a frozen lake. The ice cracked. I almost made it to shore before the Toyota went Titanic."

"You were a troublemaker, a bad boy."

"Wait, I've heard you use that phrase to describe Warrick. I'm not like him."

"Definitely not," she said. "Warrick is truly bad. He's evil. You're just…naughty. Anyway, I'm glad to hear you joking around.

"Not much of a joke," he said. "Mom didn't let me off the hook for the drowned car. The repairs cost every penny I made at my after-school job for six months. I learned my lesson."

"And that," she said, "is why you aren't like Warrick. He does awful stuff, gets away with it and never feels guilty. Not like you."

"If you say so." His tone resonated at a deeper, more intimate level. He wasn't joking anymore. When she looked up at him, peering through the morning mist, his gaze locked with hers. "Thanks, Gennie, for putting up with me."

"That's what friends do." She was accustomed to treating men like buddies, but Noah was more than a friend. "I'm here for you."

"That goes for you, too."

"Me? I'm fine."

"Yes, you are."

He reached for her through the morning mist and pulled her into an embrace. Though layers of clothing and two bullet-proof vests separated them, she felt his heart beating in time with hers. She wanted to tear off all these clothes, race back to his cabin and snuggle up in a warm, cozy bed. But they had a job to do.

His kiss was quick and perfunctory, but it still felt good.

Back in the SUV, he fired up the engine and set out for Baer's property. The rain had picked up, and they needed the windshield wipers. Thick clouds made the outlook gray and dismal, but the atmosphere inside the SUV was a hundred times more cheerful. Not only had his kiss lifted her spirits but she was glad to be taking action.

"This is so much better than staring at computer screens and reading documents," she said. "When we get to Baer's property, what should we do?"

"It depends on what's there." Noah drove with the confidence of someone who was familiar with the territory. "We'll explore, check out the area and try to find the originals that Loretta was searching for."

"Then what?"

"We'll contact Anna Rose and figure out how to pass the information about Baer to the FBI investigators without putting my neck in a noose."

"Do you really think they consider you a suspect?"

"In their shoes, I would. Check the facts—I was alone in the library with Slocum's body. I had reason to blame him for my brother's death, and that reason got deeper when we discovered that Slocum stole this land from my brother's friend. I had motive."

"So did all the other people he was blackmailing."

Among the guests at the fund-raiser, Anna Rose had identified two, possibly three, victims of Slocum's extortion schemes. If they could find the original documents and read the redacted names that had been crossed out, Gennie was certain there would be more suspects—wealthy, influential people who could lose everything if their secrets got out.

"We're almost there," he said as he turned down a rutted gravel road. "We follow this for two-point-seven miles, and then we're at Baer's property."

"Does the area look familiar to you?" She pointed through the rain at a jagged granite formation on the other side of a meadow. "That could be a landmark."

"I hate to say it, but piles of stones aren't real unusual." The SUV jostled and bounced over the ruts, forcing him to slow to a crawl. "That's why they call these mountains the Rockies."

"Nice geography lesson, smart guy."

The land on either side of the road was rugged and undeveloped. She didn't see cabins or structures of any kind. The directions Anna Rose had given them came from a BLM property map, not a postal address. Without a signpost, how would they know when they had arrived?

Noah must have been thinking the same thing because he said, "I'm guessing that there's no house on the property. And that means no search. I'm not going to dig under rocks, trying to find buried treasure."

Though she agreed with him, she wasn't ready to abandon hope. "Loretta was sure that the mountain property would provide the key. Maybe Dean told her something."

"Or she could be totally nuts." He guided the SUV onto a wide spot at the shoulder of the road. "This is two-point-seven miles."

Peering through the rain, she scanned the forested area. "There's a path leading through the trees. It looks like somebody drove a car that way."

"I'm not going to go down that so-called path with my SUV." He patted the dashboard. "She's a good car, and I don't want her to get stuck."

"As long as we're here," she said as she opened her car door, "we should check it out."

"In the rain," he muttered as he pulled up his hood.

As far as she was concerned, he had no room to complain. His weatherproof anorak would keep him nice and dry while she sopped up water like a sponge in her denim jacket. She darted into the trees, seeking shelter along the path.

About twenty yards into the forest, she spotted a small trailer camper with wheels that had gone flat a long time ago. At one time, this rusty unit had been white with blue trim. Painted in bold letters beside the door was a simple sign: Baer's Den.

She marched up to the door and yanked on the handle. "Do you remember seeing this when you came here with your brother?"

"It wasn't here. I would have remembered a nifty little hideout like this, which is probably why my brother didn't tell me about it."

The door handle was loose, and it took some jiggling to get it open. Finally she flung the door wide. The interior of Baer's Den smelled like mildew and sweaty socks. Holding her nose, she stepped aside. "You first, Noah. You said you liked the nifty hideout."

Stepping over the threshold, he barely reacted to the pungent stink. She wasn't surprised. Living in close quarters with men had led her to a theory that guys had an ability to turn off their olfactory senses. To be sure, they enjoyed pleasant fragrances, especially food aromas. But they didn't seem to be bothered by smells that made her gag.

Trying not to breathe through her nose, she followed him inside, leaving the door open. Baer's Den was a compact room with a disgusting mattress on a wooden platform, an armchair and a table that could double as a desk. Noah wasted no time going through the built-in drawers and cabinets. Without electricity, there wasn't much point in the mini-fridge or the microwave on the narrow counter beside a basin.

"Finding anything?" she asked.

"Plates, glasses and canned food," he said. "There's a bunch of raggedy old clothes in the drawers."

She bent down to peer under the platform that held the mattress and saw some half-rotted cardboard boxes. No way would she touch that stuff.

"Over here," Noah said.

In a corner under a stack of filthy pillows, there was a combination safe. Solid steel, it stood about three feet tall. She leaned down to take a closer look. "Moving this thing could be a problem. I'd estimate the weight at a hundred or a hundred and twenty pounds, and it's bolted to the floorboards. We might want to open it here. Given time, I might be able to crack the combination."

"How did you learn to do that? Were you a bank robber before you joined the military?"

"After I got good at lock-picking, I tried other stuff." She rubbed the tips of her fingers together. "I might have taken a class with a reformed burglar."

He squatted beside her and touched the face of the safe. "It doesn't look as old as the rest of the stuff in here. The trailer belonged to Baer, but I'm guessing that Slocum has been up here. He's been using this as his hiding place."

How could he stand being here? The stench was making her dizzy. "What do we do?"

"If we tear out the safe, I'm going to look even guiltier." He stood and took his cell phone from one of his many pockets. "I'm going to activate this thing and call Anna Rose."

She couldn't think of a single reason why she needed to stay in Baer's Den. She scampered past him to the door where she came to a halt. The rain had picked up. Her choices were to stay inside and deal with the stink or get drenched. She compromised by sticking her nose outside. "Hurry up, Noah."

He joined her. "It's ringing. I'll put her on Speaker."

Anna Rose popped onto his screen. She looked worried and her voice trembled. "Stop whatever you're doing. You need to find somewhere to hide until this blows over."

"We found a safe on Baer's property," Noah said.

"Listen to me. I'm more convinced than ever that this was an inside job. You can't trust anyone. My poor dear, you need to disappear."

"Explain."

"Loretta was shot. She's in critical condition."

Gennie tensed. Loretta was a difficult little woman but not someone who deserved to be attacked. "What else?"

"A witness saw someone fleeing the scene." Anna

Rose swore under her breath. "They said it was you, Noah."

Gennie barely had time to register the lie when she heard something crashing through the trees, coming at them. She drew her Beretta.

Chapter Nineteen

Noah was stunned. He was being framed for murder, another murder. His name and photo would be on the radar of every law enforcement officer in the whole damn state. And he couldn't just turn himself in and wait for justice to be done. *Trust no one.* As Anna Rose had said, he had to disappear.

He saw Gennie step through the door of the trailer, going outside into the rain. She seemed to be moving in slow motion. Her Beretta was braced in both hands. *Now what?* He watched her finger squeeze the trigger. A bullet exploded from her weapon.

The sound woke him. He stared in the direction she'd fired and saw a Hummer driving toward them on the path he hadn't wanted to take with his SUV. He shoved the phone in his pocket, pulled his Glock from the holster and stepped up beside her. "Guess I was right," he said. "Somebody was following us."

"Good instincts." She fired again—a reflex action because they both knew that her small caliber handgun wouldn't have much effect on the tank-like vehicle.

He fired as the doors to the Hummer swung open.

Two guys jumped out, guns blazing. A third and fourth emerged from the back seat.

He heard Gennie gasp, saw her stagger a step backward. "Were you hit?"

"I'm okay," she said.

"Run," he said. "Get behind the trailer and keep going."

"Not without you."

"I'll be right behind you."

He took a knee, braced his gun and laid down a steady barrage to cover her while she dodged behind the trailer. His assault had the desired result. The men who were after them ducked behind their car doors. Noah took advantage by hiding behind the edge of the trailer where he reloaded.

Peeking out, he saw the men from the Hummer creeping toward him. They were dressed in ordinary rain gear, not uniforms, and the weapons they carried weren't highly sophisticated. The guy in front looked familiar. Was he one of Murano's bodyguards?

Noah visualized his targets. He wasn't going for a kill shot, but he sure as hell wanted to slow these guys down. Taking aim, he fired five bullets in quick succession. Two men fell.

This was his chance. While the attackers were taking care of their wounded, Noah could put some distance between them and him. He weaved a path through the trees. In the distance, he squinted until he spotted Gennie. She dashed full speed, leaping over downed logs and dodging around boulders. The rain actually worked in their favor, hampering vision and making pursuit more difficult.

He'd almost caught up to her when he heard shots behind his back. He pivoted, dropped to a knee, aimed and returned fire. He realized that she was doing the same. Gennie was a sharpshooter, deadly accurate.

He heard a scream of pain. Another guy went down.

He ran those last few yards and dived behind the boulder where Gennie had taken cover. Immediately, he noticed that she was shooting one handed. "Were you hit?"

"Upper left chest but it's no big deal. Good thing I'm wearing my vest. Weird, huh? With so many parts of my body that don't feel pain, I get popped in a place that hurts like hell."

"Can you move your arm?"

She illustrated by raising it up and down. "It's stiff but I'm okay. How many of those guys are there?"

"I counted four. There might have been others in the back of the Hummer." He scanned the area, looking for the best escape. No houses, no roads, no signs of life. "I hear the creek over there. We'll go toward it."

"As if we're not wet enough already?"

He didn't have a fully formed plan, but heading toward the creek seemed like a start. The water might lead to a cabin or a road or something. This property was in the same general area as his cabin. Somehow, that had to work to his advantage.

He took off, running as fast as he could while still watching for the men who were after them. No shots were fired, but he didn't think they'd given up. They were regrouping, setting up a better strategy.

Without help, he and Gennie didn't stand a chance. There was only so long they could outrun the guys chasing them. If all the cops in the state hadn't been looking for him, Noah would have called for backup. It occurred to him that there might be a way he could reach out. He had to try.

When he got to the creek, he looked back through the forest. The men from the Hummer were still coming after them, moving cautiously. "I only see two of them."

She stood on the bank and looked down at the surging water. Spring runoff and the rain had swelled the mid-sized creek into a torrent that splashed over the bank and rushed forward, cascading over rocks and shrubs. The distance from one side to the other was about twelve feet. On the opposite bank was a rocky ledge to climb onto.

She turned to face him. "We should cross to the other side. It's going to be miserably cold and kind of dangerous, which is why I don't think they'll follow. Even if they do, the creek will slow them down."

He agreed with her logic. If he hadn't been desperate to escape, there was no way he'd jump into that churning frigid water. "I'll go first."

He stepped into the creek. First, he felt the icy cold. Then the force of the water tugged and pulled, threatening to knock him off his feet. In two steps, the creek was higher than his knees. In the middle, he was up to his hips.

He reached toward Gennie. "Take my hand."

"I can do this by myself. I don't want to throw you off-balance."

She was smaller than him and considerably lighter. He could be her anchor. "Trust me."

Without further argument, she slapped her hand into

his and held on tight. She waded forward with unsteady steps. The uneven rocks in the creek bed made it hard to walk without wobbling. Midway, the water was up to her waist.

"Come on," he encouraged her. "You can make it."

She moved cautiously. He was almost there, near enough to touch the rocky outcropping on the opposite bank.

And she slipped.

Gennie bobbed under the water. He tightened his grip, battled the force of the current and tried to pull her upright. Flailing with her free arm, she got her head above the surface. He dragged her toward the bank where he grabbed the jagged branches of a fallen pine tree. "Hang on," he urged. "You can make it."

She sank under the water again. Her grip released, and he couldn't hold onto her. She slipped from his grasp. *This can't be happening!* The rushing waters had claimed her. He stumbled back into the center of the creek, struggling to reach her as she was swept downstream.

Gasping, she rose to the surface. Her torso was out of the water. For a moment, she had regained her footing. She fought her way through the surging white water toward the bank.

He lunged toward her but couldn't get close enough. Once again, she was pulled into the current and swept away from him.

Gunfire erupted behind him. He thought the bullets sliced into the water, sending up a spray, but he couldn't tell. There was a bigger problem ahead of him. The creek roared as it narrowed to cut between two massive boulders. These were serious white-water rapids, deep and treacherous. Even if the current hadn't been intense, they couldn't escape from the water without facing a barrage of gunfire.

He crashed through the narrows, banging his hip. His head went under. He couldn't breathe. If he died, he would never forgive himself, but that wasn't the worst part. He never should have encouraged Gennie to cross the creek. She'd trusted him, and he'd led her into danger.

When he emerged, he sucked down a huge gulp of oxygen. He'd made it! The rapids were behind him. Where was Gennie? Without her, his survival meant nothing. His heart leaped when he saw her dragging herself onto a wide space at the edge of the creek.

The waters here were relatively still. He splashed up beside her, pulled her the rest of the way out and held her against him. There was no point in asking if she was all right. The creek had done a number on both of them. She was breathing hard. Her arms were limp. She must have gotten snagged on underwater rocks and branches because her cargo pants were torn in several places.

"The good news," he said, "is that the bad guys can't see us here."

"Yippee."

"But we need to move. Can you walk?"

Groaning, she forced herself to stand upright. "I can't believe it's still raining."

When she stood, he looked down at her legs and assessed her injuries. She was bleeding from a couple of slashes. "You're hurt."

"I don't feel a thing." She stared at the blood. "I'll

be okay. It's only a couple of flesh wounds. Superficial damage."

Blood oozed from the slashes. She needed medical aid. "Let me bandage your leg."

"Not now," she said. "We've got to take advantage of this break."

She was right. They needed to go. Their weapons were waterlogged and probably wouldn't be much use in a fight. They had no defense but to run as fast and as far as they could. Later, he would tend to her injuries.

She was tough and strong. A soldier who felt no pain was what he needed right now. If they got out of this alive, he intended to pamper her like a princess.

Chapter Twenty

Though the lacerations on her lower legs didn't hurt, Gennie knew the wounds were severe. The churning waters had slammed her into a submerged log with undeniable force and had dragged her against jagged slabs of granite. Her bones weren't broken, and she didn't think she had a sprain. But she was losing a lot of blood.

Under the bulletproof vest, her shoulder throbbed.

She was wet and cold, desperately cold.

Her ability to think and reason had deserted her. She was functioning on autopilot. The fact that she was still standing was a little bit miraculous, and she intended to survive. She had a will to live and a reason. Whether she liked it or not, she was in a relationship and wanted to know what was going to happen with Noah. If she died before they made love, it'd be tragic.

Slogging through the forest, she followed his instructions. He was a good leader, and she really trusted him. Not because he was her boss or because he knew his way around these forests. Her trust was a deep connection. In her heart of hearts, she knew that she'd follow this man to the end of the world. He would always be on her side and would never hurt her.

When he said run, she did her best to comply. When he told her to climb, she forced her aching muscles to hike up a steep hillside. She wished that he'd tell her to sit but understood why that order never came. If she relaxed, she doubted that she could force herself to get up.

They halted at the top of a chiseled rock cliff that was twenty-five feet above a two-lane gravel road. She wasn't sure if their position was positive or negative. The road might lead to safety. Or it might help the bad guys find them. Noah pointed to the left and said something that she didn't quite hear. She nodded anyway.

"Gennie, do you see it?"

She looked in the direction where he was pointing. "A picnic table and a trash can," she said.

"And a mile marker, it's like a map."

"Got it," she said. "We're not lost. Someone can find us."

He directed her a few steps back into the shelter of the trees, whipped off his rain jacket and spread it on the ground. "Lie down."

Gratefully, she lowered herself and sat with her legs stretched out in front of her. Blood seeped from cuts and scrapes. Her wounds looked awful, but she didn't feel much of anything. The cold made her even more numb than usual. Even her shoulder was less painful.

Noah knelt beside her. "Lay back and let me bandage you up."

She braced herself on her arms. "I don't want to be flat on my back. What if I have to run again? How will I get up?"

"We'll cross that bridge if we come to it," he said. "You need treatment. I don't want you to go into shock."

From triage training in the field, she knew the emergency treatment for shock was to have the head lower than the feet and to keep the patient warm. She really was cold, frozen to the bone. Maybe he was right about shock. "Do we have blankets?"

"I'll take care of you."

She couldn't tell what he was doing, but she saw his knife blade glistening in the rain. *Making bandages?* "Are you cutting up my cargo pants?"

"They're already ruined," he said.

But she liked these pants. And she didn't want more rain on her bare legs. Gennie knew that she should have been more concerned about the men who were shooting at them, should have been frightened. She could have died in the rapids.

But she wasn't scared.

As she watched Noah in the rain, her vision blurred. His hair was plastered to his head like a sleek sea otter. His flannel shirt was wet, clinging to his muscular arms. He had said that he'd take care of her. She'd heard those words before from other men, but she'd never believed them. Noah was different.

"What are we going to do next?" she asked.

He finished with her legs and lay beside her with his face close to hers. "I've got an idea."

A drop of rain slid down his cheek to his chin, and she wiped it away. Her hand lingered on his face. "Tell me."

"I've spent half my life in this part of the mountains. I know people who can be trusted. I'll make a call."

"Who are you calling?"

"A guy who's a retired doctor."

"What if he turns us in?"

"That's not the worst thing that could happen," he said. "If we're in custody, you'll get medical attention."

She wanted to object. Had he forgotten that this was an inside job? The inside man could be a cop. She didn't like this plan, not one bit. They could be handing themselves over to the very people who were trying to frame Noah. "I don't need a doctor. I'm feeling stronger after lying here. We can run."

He already had his phone in his hand. He'd been carrying it in a pocket inside his jacket where it wouldn't sustain too much water damage.

"I can't believe it works," she said.

"I paid extra for this protective case. If the phone is okay after the battering it took, I should send a testimonial."

He made the call. She heard him describe the area where they would wait by the picnic table and trash can. Then he lay beside her, snuggled her against him to protect her from the rain. Neither of them was warm, but when they pressed together, she was comforted. Her body began to thaw.

"It'll be about half an hour," he said.

"I trust you, Noah."

A smile lit his face. "Does that mean we're in a relationship?"

"Oh, yes. And it's going to get much better."

He gave her a squeeze. "Being that we've got men in a Hummer shooting at us and we were almost killed in creek flood, it couldn't get much worse."

But it could. What she experienced today was a walk in the park compared to the wartime detonation of explosives. She knew from her experience with Warrick that a bad relationship could kill you.

GENNIE WAKENED GRADUALLY, unsure if she was really alive or if this was part of an extended dream. She remembered being carried through a forest and riding in a car. Shivering, she recalled a terrible wet cold that permeated every cell in her body.

Now, she was blissfully warm. A comforter rested softly upon her. She wiggled into the folds and exhaled a contented groan. Without opening her eyes, she asked, "Where am I?"

"You're safe."

She wasn't surprised to hear Noah's resonant voice. His presence completed her idea of the perfect way to wake up. Slowly, she opened her eyes and saw him sitting in a chair beside the bed. "Shouldn't you be under the covers with me?"

"That's blunt, Gennie."

"If you want, I can be subtle. We can dance around each other and perform the rituals of courtship for several months. You know, dinner and dancing and movies. You can bring me flowers. I can bake you a pie. But why waste time? We both know where this is headed."

"We do," he said. "And I'm down with it."

She sat up in the bed and checked out her surroundings. The bedroom was as pink and frilly as the interior of a little girl's doll house. "You really have to tell me where we are."

"My old friend, Doc Lester, came to our rescue and brought us back here to his place. He patched up the cuts on your legs and checked your vitals. You lost a lot of blood, but you ought to be okay."

He handed her a glass of water. She drank half in one chug and gestured to the room. "Your doctor friend has strange taste."

"This is his daughter's room. She's away at college."

"I hope her major isn't fashion." Gennie assumed that the daughter was the owner of the flannel nightgown with a rosebud pattern that she was wearing. She hiked up the long hem and swung her injured legs over the edge of the bed. "What's the plan?"

"For now, we stay hidden. Doc's house is a half mile away from his nearest neighbor. Nobody knows we're here."

Keeping their whereabouts secret was wise. "Can't you use your phone? We should let Anna Rose know that Murano's men were after us."

"I never talked to you about Murano."

"You didn't need to," she said. "I recognized one of them from when we were at MIME and at the fundraiser. With all Murano's money, I wasn't surprised by the Hummer, but I thought they'd be armed with M16s. Lucky for us they stuck with handguns."

"They didn't bother to break out the major fire power." He plumped the pillows against the headboard behind her. "Didn't expect us to be much of a threat."

"Big mistake." She scooted back against the pillows and pulled the soft pink comforter over her legs, which had been stitched and swabbed with an orange antiseptic. More scars but she wouldn't think about that now. "Murano is our bad guy. He didn't actually commit the murder, but he arranged for it to happen, probably because he was being blackmailed."

"That's motive, but we still don't know exactly what Slocum had on him. The claim on the Institute's property seems likely, but there's got to be more to the story. Why would Murano resort to murder over a deed? He can afford elite lawyers. Or he could pay Slocum off."

In the back of her mind, she kept thinking of those birth certificates with no name listed for the father. If Murano once had a secret affair that resulted in a baby, his reputation would be damaged. Those twenty-eight-year-old connections might be hard to prove, but if they found the son, DNA could be compared. "Investigating the motive should be a job for the FBI."

"Already happening," he said. "Doc is driving into town to meet with Anna Rose, which is an assignment he volunteered for. I think he's got a little crush on her. And Anna Rose will report to the feds."

"Why not use the phone?"

"Maybe I'm paranoid but—as Anna Rose likes to remind me—everything can be traced. I don't want anybody finding us before we're ready to be found."

"So there's nothing we can do but wait."

"Not a bad thing. Doc said you were okay but he wanted you to rest, drink more water and eat. Sandwich?"

"And soup," she said as she leaned against the pillows.

When he leaned down to kiss her forehead, she slung an arm around his neck and pulled him closer. His lips joined with hers, and the warmth that had soothed her became a fiery heat, searing her nerve endings and making her feel alive. Her muscles quivered. The injury near her shoulder—something she'd almost forgotten—ached painfully. She gave a little cry.

"What's wrong?" he asked.

"It's the place I got shot."

He unbuttoned her nightgown and pulled it aside to reveal a giant bruise above the top of her breast. The butterfly in her tattoo looked like it was flying toward it. "Nice tat."

"It covers a scar."

"I still like it," he said. "Do you need a painkiller?"

For a moment, she considered. She was supposed to be invincible, to feel nothing. Yet, here she was with a bruise that was throbbing so hard it felt like it had a pulse. She could take meds to diminish the hurt. But she didn't want the side effects. If there were new developments, she wanted to be awake. They were still in danger. "I'm okay."

After he left the room and went downstairs to the kitchen, she got out of bed to explore. A fancy white-and-gold clock on the dresser showed the time as twenty minutes past three. From the second floor window, she saw a goat pen and a chicken coop. Though the rain had slowed to a drizzle, none of the hens were out. Only two goats roamed around their large enclosure.

On the landing outside her bedroom, she found two other bedrooms and a bathroom. Her muscles were stiff. Walking helped relax the stress, but she didn't plan to take a long hike. Twice around the landing and back to bed was plenty.

Noah returned with her soup and sandwich on a tray

with legs that he placed across her lap. "Chicken noodle and ham with cheese."

"Comfort food, that's perfect."

"And a flower," he said.

He'd added a small vase with fragrant sprigs of purple lilacs. His thoughtfulness made her smile. She liked having him take care of her. "Lilacs are one of my favorites."

"I suppose they have a meaning."

"Because they're a springtime flower, lilacs are symbolic of new love."

He nodded. "Yeah, that's what I was going for."

After she ate, he sat quietly beside her, not touching. It didn't take long for her to drift back to sleep. Resting was important. She needed to be ready if they were attacked again.

Chapter Twenty-One

Hours passed while she slept and recharged her batteries. This time, when she wakened in the fluffy, pink bedroom, her eyes opened with a snap. She was 100 percent alert and wary. As a rule, Gennie didn't pay much attention to premonitions or omens, but she trusted her gut. Something was putting her on edge. They weren't safe.

The rain had ceased, and the night was quiet. *Too quiet?* She pushed off the comforter and sat up on the bed. Through the partially open window, a fresh breeze ruffled the curtains and stirred the air. She smelled lilacs.

"Noah?" Had something happened to him? This stab of fear was irrational. "Where are you?"

She heard footsteps coming up the staircase. *Please let it be him.* Noah opened the door to her bedroom, peeked in and asked, "Are you awake?"

Relief gushed through her. Other than her overactive imagination, there was nothing to fear. She bounded from the bed into his arms. "I'm so glad you're all right."

He held her, tentatively patting her back. He must

think she was crazy, and maybe she was. Her usual self-control had lapsed, allowing her emotions to spin out of control. He squeezed her more tightly. "What's going on with you, Gennie? Two minutes ago, you were totally unconscious."

"I wake up fast." She snuggled against his chest. The soft flannel of his shirt caressed her cheek. "In a combat zone, you learn how to sleep with one eye open."

"How are you feeling?"

She hadn't bothered to take a physical inventory when she opened her eyes, but she'd managed to get out of bed without any noticeable discomfort. At the moment, her only symptom was an accelerated pulse, which was probably due to her wild emotions. "I'm okay."

"Your legs don't hurt?"

"I'm a little stiff. You probably feel the same." Stepping away from him, she turned on the bedside lamp so she could see him better. "I've been asleep for hours. Tell me what I missed."

"Doc isn't back yet. The plan is for him to stay in town tonight at Anna Rose's house. He's been calling here on the landline using some kind of encrypted phone that's untraceable. Sometimes, Anna Rose goes way over the top when it comes to crypto-security."

"Better to use too much caution than not enough." She sat on the bed beside him, thigh to thigh. The prickling along the surface of her skin had very little to do with her gut feeling about danger. She was anticipating another kind of excitement. Finally, she was in bed with Noah—a man she'd been lusting after in her fantasies. "What has Doc told you?"

"Loretta came through her surgery like a champ. She's going to be okay."

"I'm glad." And not surprised. Loretta Slocum was a tough little woman. "Did she regain consciousness? Did she tell the police who attacked her?"

"You're asking if I'm off the hook," he said. "The answer is no. Loretta was shot twice in the back. She never saw the person who pulled the trigger."

"Do we know anything more about the witness?"

"Anna Rose couldn't get her FBI contact to share that information."

"What about the lockbox at Baer's Den?" They'd risked their lives to find that safe, and she hoped their efforts had produced a significant result. "Did the FBI get that information before Murano's men could destroy it?"

"The short answer is yes."

When the dirty details of Slocum's blackmail plots were revealed, the list of real suspects would be apparent. There was no need for further investigating on their part. The ultimate solution would be up to the people who analyzed documents for the FBI. "I guess that means the case is solved."

"You'd think so," he said. "But the FBI hasn't offered to throw us a victory parade. It's going to take a while to sort out the details. Anna Rose suggested that we stay out of sight as long as possible."

Gennie could think of worse ways to spend her time. Being tucked away with Noah in a secluded mountain home on an April night after the rain sounded like heaven. She looked him up and down, from head to toe, and she fluttered her eyelashes. "What should we do to pass the time?"

"I have a few ideas."

She hopped off the bed. "Hold that thought. I'll be right back."

In the bathroom, she took a quick peek in the mirror and groaned. In the top drawer of the vanity, she found a brush, which she used in an attempt to tame her wildly curling blond hair. While washing her face, she discovered a light bruise on her chin. There were scratches on her hands, but her legs were the worst. Her encounter with the rapids had resulted in a new crop of scars. Sitting on the edge of the bathtub, she rinsed her legs, trying to remove the ugly streaks of yellow antiseptic. The stitches had been admirably done. Noah's doctor friend knew his business.

When she returned to the bedroom, he was stretched out on top of the comforter, waiting for her. He'd taken off his flannel shirt and wore a black T-shirt and jeans. She noticed that he wasn't wearing socks and shoes. His feet were long and narrow and somehow sexy. Or was that a general reflection of her mood? She hadn't been so aroused in years.

Sitting on the bed beside him, she brushed her hand over his short bristly hair. *This was happening.* A thrill went through her.

"I should warn you," she said, "you're the first man I've been with since Warrick."

"That's a long time."

"Almost three years. I haven't been avoiding sex, but I've been busy with operations, physical therapy and recovery."

"Forget about the past."

"I wish I could erase everything that happened before I met you," she said. "I'd go back in time and maybe become a virgin again."

"Do you really want that?"

She cast back to memories of her teen years when she'd been untouched and innocent. That was before life had taken a toll on her. Would she trade her experiences and her pain to be virginal again? "Probably not."

While carefully protecting the injury near her butterfly tattoo, he pulled her down beside him. When he tightened his embrace, her breasts crushed against his chest. Though he was much taller, their bodies matched nicely. His long legs entwined with hers.

At first, his kisses were light and playful. His tongue flicked into her mouth, and then he went deeper. The pressure of his lips against hers became more demanding.

She pulled back. "Not too fast."

"No problem. I like to take my time." He rearranged their positions. She was lying flat on the bed, and he hovered beside her. "You fascinate me, Gennie."

"Why?"

A wide smile spread across his face. "For one thing, you don't try to manipulate me."

"Yeah, yeah." She grinned back. "I'm blunt. You've pointed that out, maybe a thousand times."

His strong hands framed her body, outlining her waist and hips. "Do you mind if I touch your legs?"

The fresh scars weren't attractive, but she had promised herself never to be self-conscious about her injuries. And she trusted Noah. He wouldn't be disgusted by her less-than-perfect body. "Suit yourself."

He unbuttoned the flannel nightgown from the hem and eased the soft fabric up to her hips. "That's a lot of stitches."

"I got banged up pretty badly in the creek."

He stroked from her ankle to her knee. "Can you feel that?"

"This is hard to explain. I know you're touching me, but I can't tell where or how hard."

He reached around to the back of her leg and squeezed her calf. "How about that?"

"I feel it." And she liked the pressure of his hands on her legs. When his fingers glided past her knees to her thighs, she inhaled a sharp gasp. "Oh, yeah, I feel that."

When he adjusted his grasp and massaged the quads at the front of her thighs, her sensitivity was less. The nerves affecting those muscles had been seriously damaged.

Noah reached higher. His hands caressed her inner thighs. She opened her legs to him, inviting him to touch her more intimately. When he did, a tremor shook her body, and then the tremor became an earthquake. Her pent-up sensuality exploded.

Though she wasn't sure how they had both gotten undressed, it only took a moment for them to be naked together on the bed. She kissed his ear lobes, his neck and his mouth. He was a feast for her starving senses. *So handsome.* Gasping, she gazed from his dark eyes to his sensual lips and stubborn chin. *So perfectly masculine.* His body, oh, my, his body was amazing. "You have a few scars of your own," she said while she caught her breath.

"But no tats."

She guessed, "Was that another promise to your mother?"

"That's right."

"You're kind of a mama's boy." She traced a line down the center of his chest to his belly button. "I like that you're loyal to your family."

"I'm no saint," he said. "I couldn't make my marriage work."

"You have my permission to erase your past, too. Pretend that we're meeting for the first time, like a couple of virgins."

A strange fantasy because there was nothing naive or innocent about him. Frankly, she wouldn't have wanted this night to be any other way. Noah had skills that drove her to abandon her sensible inhibitions and take a chance. She might be hurt or betrayed, but she didn't believe that he'd take advantage of her trust.

Not a bad boy like Warrick, Noah was a good man.

Once they got going, she discovered talents of her own. He inspired her, aroused her and fulfilled her. When they finished with an incredible climax, she couldn't wait to do it again.

Chapter Twenty-Two

The *L* word dangled from the tip of his tongue. When Noah gazed down into her sweet, sexy blue eyes, he was dangerously close to saying it out loud, telling her that he loved her. *Maybe a giant mistake*. Though she considered trust to be more important in a relationship than love, he wasn't so sure. Trust was important, but love conquered all. Was there really a difference between the two? You couldn't have love without trust or vice versa. Too much thinking, he had to get out of his head.

He kissed the tip of her nose. "I'm going downstairs to the kitchen. Can I bring you anything?"

"I'll join you." She held the comforter over her breasts, depriving him of the charming view. "I hope I can find something to wear in here."

"Pink and frilly like a princess?"

"Doc's daughter has got to have other clothes."

"It's okay for you to stay in bed," he said. "We won't leave the house until tomorrow."

"I want to be prepared if something comes up. I should clean my weapons, dry out my hiking boots and check my supplies." She frowned. "I don't sound very romantic, do I?"

"I'm not complaining." With a body like hers, she didn't need to put on a show. She was beautiful in whatever she was wearing.

He threw on his clothes and his boots before he went downstairs. The digital clock on the stove said it was 9:27 p.m., but it felt like midnight. He looked forward to bedtime, nestled beside Gennie, feeling her smooth naked body against his. They didn't even need to have sex again, but he figured they would and he looked forward to that, too.

After rummaging in the fridge, he found bacon, eggs and bread for toast. Breakfast for dinner was one of his favorite meals. By the time he got the skillet heated, she'd joined him, wearing a pair of jeans and a sweatshirt that was—in spite of her disdain for the color—pastel pink. She sat at the table and started dissembling her weapons.

When the landline rang, he waited to hear Doc's voice on the answering machine. He owed Doc Lester a huge debt of gratitude for the rescue, patching up Gennie and giving them shelter.

"Hey, kiddo," Doc said gruffly. "Answer the phone. Where the blazes are you?"

Noah hit the button for the speakerphone. "I'm right here. How's Anna Rose?"

"She's my kind of grandma," Doc said. "And she's got another message for you. She said to tell you that the mother on the older birth certificate was almost certainly murdered."

Noah looked across the kitchen in time to catch Gennie's worried expression. Those birth certificates had been bothering her. "What brought Anna Rose to that conclusion?"

"The FBI tracked her through two identity changes to a woman who was murdered in Utah, strangled by a killer who wrapped his hands around her neck and squeezed the life out of her. He was never apprehended." Doc cleared his throat. "The typical forensic assumption is that a face-to-face strangulation involves people who know each other. It's an intimate crime because the killer can see the life draining from the victim."

Noah's gaze met Gennie's, and he saw the sadness in her eyes. She spoke up, "Hi, Doc. This is Gennie."

"Sorry about the graphic description," he said.

"I appreciate your expertise as a medical person," she said. "Did Anna Rose find out anything about the child in the birth certificate?"

"Not yet."

"Was there any new information on the more recent birth certificate?"

"Nope," he said. "And how are you feeling, young lady?"

"I'm okay," she said. "My compliments on your stitching skills."

"Don't you go running around all over the place. You lost a lot of blood and ought to take it easy. At least for a day or so."

"Yes, sir," she said.

"Same goes for you, Noah. Just relax."

"Whatever you say, Doc." The old man had known him years ago when he was a dopey teenager, tagging along behind Josh and getting into trouble. Doc had been something of a surrogate father. He taught Noah how to throw a baseball, how to fish and to shoot a rifle. "Thanks for everything."

He ended the call and returned to the stove while she finished cleaning and checking her Beretta to make sure there was no damage. "Solving the crime isn't our problem," she said, "but I can't stop thinking about it. The murder of that mother twenty-eight years ago has implications."

"What was her name on the birth certificate? Elena?"

"Suppose Murano was the guy who got her pregnant. If she approached him for child support, would he have killed her?"

"The mother of his child?" Noah hated to think of such a vile act. "We don't have enough evidence to make any kind of judgment."

"So we'll leave it to the FBI."

Through the partly open window, he heard car tires on the gravel driveway. After he moved his bacon off the flame, he took his gun from the holster on the kitchen table. "Stay here," he said to Gennie. "I'll see who it is."

"I've got your back," she promised. "Just in case, does Doc have any weapons more accurate than our handguns, like rifles?"

"In a case in the den. There's a combination lock."

As she went down the hallway, she wiggled her nimble fingers. "For me, that's not a problem."

He heard the doorbell and peeked through a window before he opened the front door for Tony Vega. "Good to see you."

"Anna Rose thought you could use a ride into town."

Tony craned his neck to look around him. "Is Gennie okay?"

Noah might have believed Tony if he hadn't just gotten off the phone with Doc. Anna Rose would have sent a message if Tony was here at her request, which meant he'd lied about his reason for being here, lied smoothly without a hint of discomfort. Noah had a bad feeling about what Tony Vega really wanted.

His first priority was to protect Gennie. Still holding his Glock, he stepped onto the porch and closed the door behind him. "Gennie's resting. She was injured today."

"Sorry to hear it."

Noah led the way as they went down the three stairs and walked toward Tony's SUV. Without being obvious, Noah scanned the road, the boulders and the surrounding trees. "Are you here alone?"

He nodded. "Can I help you pack your stuff? We should get back to Denver."

Tony was charming and handsome with his sleek black hair and his chiseled features. Noah hadn't noticed the resemblance before, but now he saw it. Tony had chocolate eyes just like his father. "How old are you, Tony?"

"Twenty-eight."

"And you're adopted, right?"

"Yes."

This was the final secret: Tony Vega was Mitch Murano's son.

Before he was murdered, Dean Slocum had created a complicated mystery of twists and turns and clandestine information. He went from blackmail to property fraud with Baer and Murano. Then he uncovered the final secret about Tony's birth.

Noah stared hard at the young man he'd worked with and said, "The FBI is tracking information on your birth mother. The name on your birth certificate was Elena. She had to change it twice."

"I don't know what you're talking about." He shrugged. "The only thing I know about my birth mother is that she gave me up for adoption. The Vegas were nice people, but I was destined for greater things."

"Like Slocum's murder?"

The direct accusation struck home. Tony drew his weapon. They stood only a few feet apart with their guns trained on each other.

"You figured it out," Tony said. "Do you also understand that Slocum had it coming? He was an extortionist, a liar, a cheat."

"So you and Warrick killed him. You were the inside man. How did you get into the library?"

"After I disabled the surveillance camera outside the library, I faked an emergency with a drunk at the front entrance. That gave me an excuse to change clothes after the murder. I hid in the library and appeared when Gennie opened the door."

"Why now?" Noah asked. "It seems like Slocum has been blackmailing your father for a long time. Did he uncover something that was more of a threat?"

"Now that my father is running for office, his reputation is more important. Also, there's the matter of the second birth certificate. That's my daughter. I want her to have a better life than I did, and that means introducing her to her grandfather. He owes me."

It didn't sound like Tony was real fond of Murano, but Noah didn't make the mistake of playing on his loyalties or friendship. "Why did you frame me?"

"I plan to take over your job, but that's not the most important reason. After I start working for my father, I can pick whatever I want to do."

"Why me?"

His eyes were cold, uncaring. "You were convenient."

"I'm guessing that you were the witness who supposedly saw me shoot Loretta."

"Right again, Noah. You aren't as dumb as you look." His whitened teeth flashed in a harsh smile. "Or maybe you are. Either way, you need to come with me."

"Why would I do that?"

"Remember when I said I was alone? Well, buddy, I lied. I brought two guys from my father's security team. After the hassle at the creek, they don't like you or Gennie very much. If I give them any excuse at all, they'll open fire."

Noah figured a shootout wouldn't end well for anybody. He needed a better plan, some kind of leverage. He took a calculated guess. "How much backup do you need?"

"What do you mean?"

Noah nodded toward the SUV. "Who's in the car?"

A door to the back seat swung open, and Murano stepped out. His melodious voice contrasted his ruthless words. "Kill this man, Tony. We have a defense. According to evidence, Noah killed Slocum and shot Loretta. If he's dead, the investigation will go away."

"Here's the deal," Noah said. "I'll go with you, but you have to leave Gennie alone."

"No can do," Murano replied. "Gennie has to die. She's your alibi for last night."

"Not really," he said. "I had time to get into town and back to the cabin without her knowing. We didn't sleep in the same bed last night."

Tony laughed. "You're pathetic."

"Let me tell Gennie to stay here, and we'll be on our way." Noah doubted this plan would work. Tony clearly didn't have a problem lying to him, but he had to try something. He loved this woman and would do anything to give her a fighting chance. He placed his Glock on the ground. "I'll come quietly."

"Sure, why not?"

"Don't fall for this," Murano said. "Shoot them both. Do it now."

A look of disgust flashed across Tony's face. He turned away from his father and raised his voice. "Hey, Gennie, it's Tony. Come out here."

She stepped through the front door. In the pink sweatshirt, she seemed young and vulnerable. Her hand raised and she waved. "Hi, Tony. Dr. Murano."

Without letting him respond, Noah said, "Gennie, you need to stay here. No matter what happens, stay in the house. Don't ask me why. You have to do it."

"That's unreasonable." She arched an eyebrow. "What if I want to go into town? You can't just tell me it's all for the best and I should trust you."

"This isn't about trust." His plan to rescue her at any cost wasn't about promises he might have made. Sacrificing himself for her safety was about something bigger and more important. "It's about love."

She eased toward the open door. "They say the greatest love is between a mother and child. Do you agree with that, Tony?"

He raised his gun and pointed it at her. "You don't know what you're talking about."

"Her name was Elena. Do you remember her at all, the woman who gave birth to you? She tried to protect you, but she was no match for Murano. Your father killed her, Tony. Strangled her and watched as she died."

Tony cried out. He pivoted and aimed his weapon at his father.

Noah saw Gennie dive through the door into the safety of the house. This was his chance to bring this danger to an end.

GENNIE DASHED THROUGH the house with a clear plan. Noah loved her, and she'd be damned if she let that go. In an upstairs window, she'd set up a sniper's nest with two rifles she'd taken from Doc's gun cabinet. Her training as a sharpshooter was about to pay off.

Below her, she saw Tony fire a shot at Murano who went down. Noah used the distraction to attack Tony. They wrestled for the gun. No way could she risk a shot at Tony without putting Noah in danger. Besides, there was another threat.

She'd listened to every word that passed between Tony and Noah. She knew that two of Murano's men were hiding in the area. Using the long-distance scope on the rifle, she spotted two shooters in the trees at the edge of Doc's property. They were careless, didn't expect to take fire. In minutes, she managed clean shots on both of them. Then she came around to Tony. That little snake, how could he betray Noah? At least, he'd reacted like a decent person when he heard that his father had strangled his mother.

Before she could get off a shot, Noah had him down on the ground with his hands zip-tied behind his back. She picked up the landline and called nine-one-one before she flew down the staircase into the front yard.

When she threw herself into Noah's arms, her bruise ached. She felt the pain and accepted it. Some things in life were going to hurt. Others were pure pleasure.

She heard police sirens in the distance. "I love you, Noah."

He kissed her. "And yet, you disobeyed my order to go back in the house and sit tight."

"Well, excuse me for saving you."

"Good point." He kissed her again. "I want to offer you a permanent position."

"With ARC?"

"With me," he said. "I want to wake up with you every morning, and tuck you into bed every night. Let me love you twenty-four-seven."

"I accept."

She couldn't think of anywhere else she'd rather be.

* * * * *

COMING NEXT MONTH FROM

(H) HARLEQUIN

INTRIGUE

Available February 18, 2020

#1911 BEFORE HE VANISHED
A Winchester, Tennessee Thriller • by Debra Webb
Halle Lane's best friend disappeared twenty-five years ago, but when
Liam Hart arrives in Winchester, Halle's certain he's the boy she once knew.
As the pair investigates Liam's mysterious past, can they uncover the truth
before a killer buries all evidence of the boy Halle once loved?

#1912 MYSTERIOUS ABDUCTION
A Badge of Honor Mystery • by Rita Herron
Cora Reeves's baby went missing in a fire five years ago, but she's convinced
the child is still out there. When Sheriff Jacob Maverick takes on the cold
case, new leads begin to appear—as well as new threats.

#1913 UNDERCOVER REBEL
The Mighty McKenzies Series • by Lena Diaz
Homeland Security agent Ian McKenzie has been working undercover
to break up a human-trafficking ring, but when things go sideways,
Shannon Murphy is suddenly caught in the crosshairs. Having only recently
learned the truth about Ian, can Shannon trust him with her life?

#1914 SOUTH DAKOTA SHOWDOWN
A Badlands Cops Novel • by Nicole Helm
Sheriff Jamison Wyatt has spent his life helping his loved ones escape his
father's ruthless gang. Yet when Liza Dean's sister finds herself caught in the
gang's most horrifying crime yet, they'll have to infiltrate the crime syndicate
and find her before it's too late.

#1915 PROTECTIVE OPERATION
A Stealth Novel • by Danica Winters
Shaye Geist and Chad Martin are both hiding from powerful enemies in the
wilds of Montana, and when they find an abandoned baby, they must join
forces. Can they keep themselves and the mysterious child safe—even as
enemies close in on all sides?

#1916 CRIMINAL ALLIANCE
Texas Brothers of Company B • by Angi Morgan
There's an algorithm that could destroy Dallas, and only FBI operative
Therese Ortis and Texas Ranger Wade Hamilton can find and stop it. But
going undercover is always dangerous. Can they accomplish their goal
before they're discovered? _____

**YOU CAN FIND MORE INFORMATION ON UPCOMING HARLEQUIN TITLES,
FREE EXCERPTS AND MORE AT HARLEQUIN.COM.**

HICNM0220

SPECIAL EXCERPT FROM

(H)HARLEQUIN

INTRIGUE

Sheriff Jamison Wyatt has never forgotten Liza Dean, the one who got away. But now she's back, and she needs his help to find her sister. They'll have to infiltrate a crime syndicate, but once they're on the inside, will they be able to get back out?

Read on for a sneak preview of
South Dakota Showdown *by Nicole Helm.*

Chapter One

Bonesteel, South Dakota, wasn't even a dot on most maps, which was precisely why Jamison Wyatt enjoyed being its attached officer. Though he was officially a deputy with the Valiant County Sheriff's Department, as attached officer his patrol focused on Bonesteel and its small number of residents.

One of six brothers, he wasn't the only Wyatt who acted as an officer of the law—but he was the only man who'd signed up for the job of protecting Bonesteel.

He'd grown up in the dangerous, unforgiving world of a biker gang run by his father. The Sons of the Badlands were a cutthroat group who'd been wreaking havoc on the small communities of South Dakota—just like this one—for decades.

Luckily, Jamison had spent the first five years of his life on his grandmother's ranch before his mother had fully given in to Ace Wyatt and moved them into the fold of the nomadic biker gang.

Through tenacity and grit Jamison had held on to a belief in right and wrong that his grandmother had instilled in him in those early years. When his mother had given birth to son after son on the inside of the Sons, Jamison had known he would get them out—and he had, one by one—and escape to their grandmother's ranch situated at the very edge of Valiant County.

HIEXP0220

It was Jamison's rough childhood in the gang and the immense responsibility he'd placed on himself to get his brothers away from it that had shaped him into a man who took everything perhaps a shade too seriously. Or so his brothers said.

Jamison had no regrets on that score. Seriousness kept people safe. He was old enough now to enjoy the relative quiet of patrolling a small town like Bonesteel. He had no desire to see lawbreaking. He'd seen enough. But he had a deep, abiding desire to make sure everything was right.

So it was odd to be faced with a clear B and E just a quarter past nine at night on the nearly deserted streets. Maybe if it had been the general store or gas station, he might have understood. But the figure was trying to break into his small office attached to city hall.

It was bold and ridiculous enough to be moderately amusing. Probably a drunk, he thought. Maybe the…woman—yes, it appeared to be a woman—was drunk and looking to sleep it off.

When he did get calls, they were often alcohol related and mostly harmless, as this appeared to be.

Since Jamison was finishing up his normal last patrol for the night, he was on foot. He walked slowly over, keeping his steps light and his body in the shadows. The streets were quiet, having long since been rolled up for the night.

Still, the woman worked on his doorknob. If she was drunk, she was awfully steady for one. Either way, she didn't look to pose much of a threat.

He stepped out of the shadow. "Typically people who break and enter are better at picking a lock."

The woman stopped what she was doing—but she hadn't jumped or shrieked or even stumbled. She just stilled.

Don't miss
South Dakota Showdown *by Nicole Helm,*
available March 2020 wherever
Harlequin Intrigue books and ebooks are sold.

Harlequin.com